Under the Aurora Sky

ELISSA DAYE
KAREN FULLER

World Castle Publishing, LLC
Pensacola, Florida
Copyright © 2022 Shein Partnership, LLC
Authors: Melissa Davis & Karen Fuller
Hardback ISBN: 9798849834931
Paperback ISBN: 9781958336687
eBook ISBN: 9781958336694
First Edition World Castle Publishing, LLC, September 20, 2022
http://www.worldcastlepublishing.com

Chapter 1

Isaak Lee released a frustrated sigh as he glared at his computer screen. This article just didn't sound like him. It read more like a news report than the nature article he was supposed to be writing. It didn't seem to matter how many times he rewrote it, either. It seemed to be missing something, but what? At this rate, he'd be the laughing stock of the office. In his ten-year writing career, Isaak had never had this much trouble before coming up with the right words. When, in fact, he had several plaques hanging in his office cubicle for all the prize-winning magazine articles he'd written.

He leaned back in his office chair, closed his eyes and reached up, pinching the bridge of his nose, hoping to relieve the tension headache suddenly there. Something had to give, and he hoped it wasn't his job.

Dammit, this wasn't like him. It certainly wasn't where he had started, either. His aspirations had led him down a different path. Isaak was born and raised in Toronto. He knew every nook and cranny of the city and could write about anything going on there. The assignment didn't matter. The words would flow like magic from his fingers as they danced over the keyboard onto the screen. At his former job, every article Isaak put out was gold for the magazine until he dug too deep and embarrassed a high-ranking official. It was all true, but his former boss didn't like the heat. It cost Isaak his job and his reputation. His dreams of furthering his success in the world of journalism were scattered like dust in the wind.

Now, there he sat, in a small cubicle working for a wildlife magazine of all places. Not exactly his dream job, but after the debacle at the other magazine, the industry had blackballed him. He was lucky his cousin had connections. If not, Isaak would be fortunate to be an advisor at a high school newspaper, let alone continue to write freelance anywhere in the world.

Frustration washed over him again. Dammit, he was a good reporter, but he was way out of his element here. What did he know about fishing, or any kind of nature, for that matter? Not much, and faking it didn't seem to work well for him either. He was like a fish out of water, trying to prove that he could survive on land when he was desperate to get back to the water where he belonged. At this rate, if he made it through the next week, he'd be lucky.

He reached for his mouse again. Maybe if he did more research on fishing, it would help him with his article. The best way to pretend to be an expert was to at least have some kind of knowledge of the topic at hand. Fly fishing? What the hell was that anyway? Did they fish for flies or use flies for bait?

"A word?"

Isaak sat up straight and tried not to cringe. It was his boss, Angel Dawson. The woman was all business, and the only reason she'd hired him in the first place was that she was married to his cousin. Even in her late sixties, the woman was still at the top of her game, and if she didn't think Isaak was pulling his weight, she wouldn't hesitate to fire him, and he knew it.

Isaak swallowed hard before plastering on a well-practiced smile and turning to face her. "Sure. How can I help you?"

Angel raised an eyebrow and looked at him through the horn-rimmed glasses perched on the tip of her nose. If her expression were any indication, Isaak's charm wasn't working on her.

"My office." Angel didn't wait for him to respond before heading to her office.

Odds of him charming his way out of this? Not a chance in hell. Isaak's heart sank as he watched her brisk retreat. That well-practiced smile faded to be replaced by a worried grimace. If she fired him now, it would be the record for the shortest time on a job for him.

Grabbing his suit jacket from the back of the chair and straightening his tie, Isaak resolved he'd go with as much dignity as possible. Maybe all wasn't lost — yet.

Isaak took a deep breath before raising his hand to knock on the doorframe. The door was open, but he didn't want to just barge in. He had made that mistake before. It wasn't one he would likely make again.

Angel looked up from the article she was reading, motioned him to come in, and gestured toward a chair across from her desk. "Sit, Mr. Lee."

Her refusal to acknowledge him by his first name bothered him on many levels. Here goes nothing, he thought as he gave her another practiced smile. "No Isaak? Not using my first name must mean I'm in trouble. Lay it on me, Angel."

Angel clasped her hands in front of her on the desk. "Look, Isaak, I took you in here because you were a highly qualified journalist. Your awards speak for themselves."

Isaak braced himself, waiting for the other proverbial shoe to drop. "Why do I feel like there's a but coming in there somewhere?"

"You are also highly intuitive." She picked up the article again and gestured with it. "You are one of our most talented writers, but you lack experience." She put the article back down on her desk. "That is a problem for this magazine."

Isaak knew the article in front of her was his. The one he'd just been fretting over. Maybe he could still salvage this. "I have plenty of experience. My record speaks for itself, Angel."

Angel nodded. "I'm not criticizing your writing, Isaak. You're just lacking in the nuances that our readers require."

That was a new one. If she didn't have a problem with his writing, then he didn't understand how else he could be lacking. And how could she know what the readers thought of his writing? Had she taken an actual poll? Whatever. He needed this job and would put in the effort. "What do you mean?"

Angel gestured to her walls and bookshelf. "Tell me, Issak, what do you see when you look around my office?"

Was this a trick question? He glanced around the office. The walls were covered with nature scenes. The bookshelves held awards and wildlife statues. "Nature and wildlife?"

Angel nodded. "Have you ever set foot inside the woods? Gone hunting? Fishing? Or even camping, for that matter?"

"I've fished before." Isaak shrugged. Well, just a little, and never fly fishing, or he would actually understand what that meant.

Somewhat amused, Angel shook her head. "Casting your rod into a small pond at a park fishing tournament as a child does not count."

She remembered. Isaak grinned. "Hey, you went to the same one, Angel."

"I did," Angel smirked. "I also remember I had to bait your hook for you." The smile dropped from Isaak's face. "Look, Isaak, you know I love you."

"You married my cousin, you kind of have to."

She gave him an indulgent smile. "And it's because of him that I gave you a job here. I know life hasn't been easy for you lately. You needed a place to start over."

"But...?"

"Again, you are very intuitive." Angel sat forward in her chair. "I need someone who can roll up their sleeves and get down and dirty."

He didn't understand. The last time he wrote down and dirty, he got fired. "I'm not sure what you're getting at."

"Isaak, you write articles about exploring some of the most beautiful places in the world, but you write like an outsider. I need you to write as if you've been there, experienced it, lived in that moment." She took a deep breath before continuing. "Our readers are looking for an escape, and they're looking at you to provide that for them. To let them experience it through your eyes."

"And you think I can't do that?" What did she want him to do, write fiction? He was a journalist, not a hobby novelist. He wrote the facts, not some fluff piece that marginalized his abilities.

Angel sat back in her chair. "Right now, no." She threw out her hand to make a point. "I know your background, Isaac. You grew up here in Toronto. You know your way around town. This is your comfort zone." She shook her head with regret. "The old adage is to write what you know. And, frankly, if I were asking you to write articles about the city, we wouldn't be sitting here right now. But this magazine isn't about the city, it's about nature and wildlife. Two things you have little to no experience with."

"Are you firing me?" Isaak swallowed hard. There was no argument there. She was right, but dammit, he needed this job. He inwardly cringed, waiting for her answer.

"No, not if you get a handle on things." A ghost of a smile formed on her lips. "And I have just the thing to help you."

Okay, so he wasn't fired, at least not yet. Maybe he could work with this. He was willing to do whatever it took, well, almost anything. Isaak drew the line at eating exotic food like chocolate-covered or deep-fried bugs or anything along that line. He was not one of those men who would ever put himself on a quest to taste things that humans should never eat, nor could he see himself conquering any unwanted fears anytime soon. People who sought those adventures were just adrenaline junkies. Just thinking about it was bad enough. Part of him worried that this might be exactly the kind of thing Angel was talking about, though.

"What's that?" Isaak braced himself, almost afraid of the answer.

"I'm going to send you on a special assignment."

"Where exactly?" He felt his stomach drop to the bottom of his feet. Isaak had a bad feeling about this. Was she going to send him to the top of Mount Kilimanjaro?

"The Great Bear Rainforest. I assume you have

heard of it."

Isaak hesitated. "I know it's one of the largest rainforests on Earth. Why do you want me to go there?"

Angel gave him a bright smile. "Experience real-life exploration. Find your primitive self. Learn to speak to our readers in a language only they understand."

"A modern-day walkabout?" Part of him was relieved that it wasn't nearly as far away as Tanzania and he would still be on the same continent, but that was only a small relief. It would still take him far out of the city.

"Precisely. I've already made all the arrangements."

His mind raced. Arrangements? He'd never even been camping, and she wanted him to be a real-life Daniel Boon? Was this job even worth it? He thought hard about it. It was if he didn't want to be eating ramen noodles for the rest of his life, he'd better give it a shot. "So I have to go?"

"You do know the National Magazine Awards are coming up, right?" Isaak inclined his head. He hadn't given the award much thought other than the deadline for entries was next spring. "Wildlife

Adventures is counting on you to bring it home. What better way to prove your worth to the magazine?"

His stomach wrenched in a tight knot. Not only was she expecting him to go on some crazy camping expedition, but she was expecting a prize-winning story out of it, too. What choice did he have? None, really. Not if he wanted to keep his job. "No pressure there."

"You're a seasoned reporter, Isaak. I know you can do this. I've seen what you can do when you're passionate about something. Get passionate about this and make our magazine proud."

"I will." He wished he could make his voice sound confident. The truth was, he'd be lucky to pull this off without screwing it all up. As much as Isaak wished he could turn away from this place, it was the only place left for him. Besides, he wasn't raised to be a quitter. There was only one thing to do. Suck it up and put his best foot forward.

"That really didn't sound very enthusiastic. We need you to give it your all. I need this." She gave him a pointed look. "You need his too if you want to keep your job here at the magazine."

"I'll psych myself up for it. You can count on me, Angel. I just have to let all this process."

"You see that you do, young man." She stacked the papers on her desk, putting them in a neat pile before her. "Take the rest of today off. Get your bags packed. You leave tomorrow morning. I'll have my secretary email you your itinerary."

"Fine."

Isaak felt the weight of the world on his shoulders as he rose from the chair and headed for the door. Just what had he gotten himself into?

"And, Isaak?"

He braced himself as he turned to look back at her. He was usually a very confident man, but right now, he felt like a chastised child being thrown to the big bad wolf. "Yes, Angel?"

"Don't come back without the story of a lifetime."

His stomach did an involuntary flip-flop, but he put on his game face to hide his inner turmoil. "I will, boss. You can count on me."

Chapter 2

Isaak stopped at a local sporting goods store on his way home. He had no choice. He couldn't very well traipse around in the woods in an Armani suit and a silk tie. Instead, he looked for everything that would help him survive a few days in the woods. The man at the register gave him a bizarre look as he checked out, but Isaak had pushed past the awkwardness of the moment and did his best to ignore him. He was not happy that this trip was costing him a small fortune, and he hadn't even left yet.

Ladened down with three huge shopping bags of survival gear and clothes, Isaak made it through the front door of his posh, upscale apartment. He tossed his keys into a bowl on a table by the door and made his way into the bedroom.

Isaac's bedroom was a modern contemporary. In the middle of the back wall sat a king-sized platform bed with a brown upholstered headboard. The bed coverings and pillows were in assorted earth tones. He was a modern man, happy with his one-bedroom apartment in the city. It was just a small shot to his work and close to everything he needed, so he didn't have to spend too much of his off time driving around running errands.

Isaak reached over and turned on the lamp sitting on the nightstand next to the bed. The room flooded with light. As he was reaching into the top of his closet for the luggage, his cell phone rang. Looking down at the number, he smiled to himself. Damned if she wasn't right on time, as usual. "Hi, Mom, what's up?"

"You better tell me it's just a nasty rumor, Isaak, or I swear I'll—"

Concerned, Isaak sat down on the edge of the bed. "Hold on, Mom. What rumor?"

"Your cousin called—"

Boy, news traveled fast in this town. "Okay, Mom, that is true, but—"

His mother interrupted him. "I can't believe Angel is sending you out to the middle of nowhere."

"I'm a grown man. I'll be all right." At least, that was what he tried to tell himself. Who knows what he had really gotten himself into by agreeing to this trip? He could only hope it didn't involve eating grubs off some logs or something disgusting like that. The furthest he had been willing to test his palette was the escargots he'd had three years ago. Never again. Give him some babyback ribs any day, dry rub or barbecue. He could eat those babies anyway which way they spiced them, so long as they had some flavor and fell off the bone.

"You don't have to keep reminding me that you're grown. I'm well aware of that, son. But I'm a mother, and mothers still worry about their unmarried sons. It's ingrained in our DNA."

Isaak smiled. "You'd worry more if I lost my job."

"Don't get me started with that one. Are you sure you don't want me to talk to Nicki?"

Isaak got up to pace. Great. She really was wound up. He could see her head bobbing through the phone. This was not going to end well for him if he didn't find a way to appease her soon. She'd call someone else on the phone chain, and then he'd be dealing with even more drama. "I don't need Cousin Nicki to fight my battles. It's bad enough that everyone thinks I got handed this job because I'm family."

She grunted into the phone. "That's not the only reason you got the job. You're a highly qualified professional, Isaak."

"Yes, but Angel's right. My readers want more reality in my writing." He hadn't been surprised by his dressing down, really. Isaak knew his writing wasn't getting it done, but he was not about to give up yet. Maybe he just needed to challenge himself more. Isaak wasn't sure if it was because he had lost his oomph or he had taken the wrong job. The problem was that there hadn't been any other jobs that met his qualifications. Isaak didn't need to start over from scratch. He had already spent his time in the trenches and wasn't ready to stoop to writing for a sleazy tabloid or rag magazine. He'd have to be desperate to even consider that.

"Are you sure you wouldn't rather find another job that doesn't send you out into the wild?" Isaak could tell she was giving in, but he still heard the worry in her voice.

Isaak put the cell phone on speaker and started packing. He knew she wasn't going to let this go easily. "It's Vancouver, Mother. It's not like I'm being left in the Serengeti. Besides, I'll have a guide with me at all times."

"I still don't like it. Roughing it in the wild."

"You make it sound like I won't be able to handle it." Isaak frowned when his mother didn't respond right away. What did that say about him? Did she think he was some limp noodle who couldn't take care of himself? It was just a hike. Not like they were going big cat hunting or something. Not that idea was appealing to him, either. "You do think that. Admit it."

"I think you're many things, baby. Outdoor explorer, it's just not one of them."

So, there he had it. Her confidence in his abilities was waning quickly. If he didn't do something about that real quick, she'd start demanding he move back home so she could take care of her baby and giving up his bachelor lifestyle wasn't something he would be doing anytime soon. While the rest of his cousins had all started settling down, Isaak had strayed far from that pack. He had been too focused on his career and living life with no strings tying him down. Maybe his lack of a long-term anything made his mom feel like his life was a little on the rocks. Even so, he'd always been able to take care of himself.

Isaak imagined that Angel and Nicki were already taking bets as to how long he would last on this adventure or if he would manage to come back in one piece. He could see their amused faces now, and he tried to push that image aside. The more he thought about it, the more resolved he was. He'd have to prove to everyone that he wasn't just some city slicker. He could take care of himself. "Guess I have to prove myself to a lot of people."

"Baby, I didn't mean to hurt your feelings. It's just—"

"I need to finish packing, Mom. I'll let you know when I get back." If he didn't cut this short, he would never get her off the phone. When she went on a tangent, she was like a cat chasing a red laser, not letting it out of her sight for anything. Isaak just didn't have the energy for it tonight, especially since his flight left so early in the morning.

"You better. Better yet, call me every day, so I know you're all right. If something happens to you, I'll never forgive Angel."

"I doubt there'll be too many cell towers out there, but I'll call you when I can. Bye, Mom."

Isaak tossed the phone on the bed and shook his head. "Does everyone think I'm incompetent? It's just a few days in the woods. What's the worst that can happen?"

Ticks, leeches, fungal infections? Apparently, late-night internet searches were not very helpful. They always had people finding the worst things. It was probably best that he keep his phone on the charger instead of thumbing through unnecessary tidbits for the rest of the night. That would definitely lead to insomnia, and right now, that was something he didn't need. Tomorrow would be here before he knew it, and he would much rather face it with a reasonably rested mind that could actually spit a few rational thoughts. Otherwise, he'd be jacked up on coffee, and his mind would be spinning out of control.

Just as he was about to turn in for the night, his phone dinged again. Looking down at the phone, he saw Kat's text pop across the screen. He knew that she was going to be irritated with him. Hell, he was used to that by now. Something always got under that woman's skin. First, it was refusing to make them an official item. Isaak had tried to tell her he wasn't looking for a plus one on any of his dance cards, but she didn't want to take no for an answer. She had become his occasional plus one when the moment called for it or when either one of them was ready for something a little more casual to keep them satisfied.

You could be here. Kat sent a photo of the empty side of the bed.

Sorry, work calls. Isaak saw the next photo with the red lace lingerie peeking through, and he groaned. She was not playing fair. That was Kat for you. She was a woman who knew what she wanted. Fine, young, everything that would keep a young brother happy, but Kat wasn't the kind of girl one brought home to his mother. And he wasn't interested in anything long-term with anyone, so the two of them had an open relationship. No strings at all. She was allowed to go out with whomever she wanted to, and so was he. Casual. That was all he was interested in. He knew his mother was anxious for him to settle down and start providing her with grandkids, but Isaak was just not interested in that at this point in his life.

All work and no play.

Good night, Kat. Isaak turned his phone off. He knew she would keep messaging him if he left it on. That was her pattern. It would piss her off for a little while to be ignored, but eventually, she would get over it and call him back. Honestly, if she didn't, the world wouldn't end for him. Isaak wasn't in the market for anything permanent. Right now, he just wanted to keep his career out of the toilet. Focusing on anything else would be a distraction.

Isaak double-checked his bags one last time before setting the alarm on his phone. He pulled back the covers and slid underneath. When his head hit the pillow, he knew it was going to be one of those nights. Flipping on the flat screen tv, he turned something on that would be easy to fall asleep to, for he rarely could fall asleep without some kind of background noise to distract him. Growing up, they had lived closer to the highway, which was always filled with driving noises of one kind or another.

The city was always filled with enough noise to keep his brain distracted at night. Tonight, it was his thoughts that distracted him. Maybe he had made the wrong choice in not seeing Kat tonight. She'd at least help him blow off some of this steam. It would have allowed him to fall asleep faster, but it might have kept him up too late as well. Deciding to be responsible was the right choice for a change. Instead, Isaak watched the late-night show until his eyelids started to drift shut.

Chapter 3

The flight to Vancouver was uneventful, as far as flights were concerned these days. Thankfully, he got there on time. While he didn't get a crap ton of sleep, the caffeine he had guzzled on the way to the airport had helped him keep focused enough to get to where he needed to be on time. So far, everything was going to plan, whatever Angel's plan happened to be. He was barely clued into the plans, flying by the seat of his pants, but what else could he do?

After Isaak picked up his rental car, he set the GPS to find the Blue Moon Bar and Grill. That was where he was supposed to be meeting up with his guide. Some guy by the name of Danny. He wasn't looking forward to the meeting, mostly because he wasn't sure what kind of backwater ruffian he'd be running into. Isaak was all city through and through. The idea of proving his manliness in the great outdoors didn't appeal to him, nor did beating his chest like some neanderthal to show just how strong and capable he was. He only hoped his guide was old enough to not make him feel like some junior was leading him around. Then again, having some grandpa tell him how to do things might not be great, either.

There was no way around it. Isaak was just plain screwed. One way or the other, he was going to look like a fish out of water. He might as well lean into it and get it over with. He turned on the radio and flipped through the stations until he found something that would distract him from his thoughts. From there, he just focused on the drive. As he drove along, he found the scenery changing from small cityscape to more outback country. It should have surprised him, but it didn't. This was an outdoor expedition of sorts. Of course, Angel would send him out to the middle of nowhere. Okay, it wasn't the middle of nowhere. It was just less interesting to him because the world he was used to had a skyline filled with the tops of skyscrapers.

Finally finding his destination, he pulled into the dimly lit parking lot. The Blue Moon Bar was a bar and grill attached to a small two-story hotel. Several cars were parked in the parking lot. Isaak pulled into the first available spot. Looking up at the bar, he took in the view. It was rustic, a little back woodsy for his taste, even from the outside. The windows were illuminated with dimly lit light from the inside and the neon light from the sign hanging over the door.

To say Isaak was a little nervous about this expedition was an understatement. What lay ahead was way outside his comfort zone, but what choice was there? None that he could see. He didn't know any man who wanted to have his weaknesses put on display for someone else's entertainment. He was certainly not keen to do so, but he also didn't want to lose his job. Maybe he should just look at this as the learning opportunity it was intended to be. Buck up, so to speak. If he didn't find a way to do so, he might lose his job, and he didn't want to go back to writing for some low-budget city paper that couldn't even bother to spell-check its journalists.

I'll just go inside, meet this Danny, and hopefully, the man will understand I'm a novice and, and, and what? he thought. He'll think you're an idiot, that's what. What grown man doesn't know his way around the woods? This one, that's who. Go with plan B. You'll just march right in there and take charge. That's right, take charge. Grab the bull by the horns and hold on for dear life. Fake it till you make it.

As Isaak approached the entrance, the music from the jukebox thrummed with a bit of bass. Several loud conversations were going on inside. The sounds of pool balls clacking and boisterous laughter greeted him. Not quite the sounds he was used to. Isaak spent most of his time in clubs where the music pumping through the speakers was like a heartbeat that moved the crowd around him.

Isaak stepped through the entrance. Just inside the door, the bar, a rustic hardwood, stretched out before him. The top was of polished wood and had several barstools lining the front.

Several booths filled with patrons lined the two outer walls, and small tables were spread out in the middle of the room. Toward the back of the room stood two pool tables with games in progress. It was pretty much a standard bar, less upscale than some he'd stepped into before, but it definitely reminded him of his collegiate days. Isaak pulled out a stool and took a seat at the bar.

Behind the bar was a man who looked to be in his late fifties. He was of medium athletic build, dark-complected with long black hair that he wore in a ponytail in the back. He was drying glasses and putting them away behind the bar.

The bartender placed a bowl of peanuts in front of Isaak. "What can I get for you?"

"Whatever's on tap."

"No Problem." The bartender poured the beer and placed it on a napkin in front of Isaak.

"Thanks." Isaak took a small sip of the beer as he looked around the room.

"You're not from around here," the man concluded as he studied Isaak.

Here we go. Isaak gave him a self-conscious smile. "How can you tell?"

The man chuckled to himself. "You got a city-slicker vibe. Where ya from?"

Oh, boy. So much for faking it. Would Danny size him up just as easily? "I'm from Toronto."

Giving Isaak a dubious look, he said, "What brings you to our neck of the woods?"

"I'm on assignment." Isaak glanced around the room, then turned back to the bartender. "Speaking of which, I'm supposed to meet Danny here. Do you know where I can find him?"

"Dani?" He gave a derisive snort. His eyes twinkled with mischief. "I'll make sure *he* knows you're here."

Speaking of vibes, something was definitely up with this dude. He seemed to be having too much fun at his expense. Why, he had no idea, but it sure put Isaak on the offense. Isaak watched the man enter the back room and tried to tell himself he was just imagining things. This whole situation made him a lot more sensitive than usual, and it wasn't a good look.

A few seconds later, a beautiful waitress exited the back room and slid behind the bar. Isaak gave her an appreciative once over as she walked toward him. She was of medium height, in her early thirties, with high cheekbones and almond-shaped eyes. Isaak admired her slim, athletic figure in her tight jeans and t-shirt. She wore her long black hair in a loose braid. The waitress was strikingly attractive. Any man would have been blind not to notice her.

"Can I help you?"

Isaak glanced from his full glass back to her. "I've already got a drink, but thanks."

The woman narrowed her eyes at him, and for some reason, that made her prettier to Isaak. He smiled at her and wondered if he had time to talk her up while he waited for Danny to get here. Not that he was looking for a hook-up right now, but he could use a friendly face to pass the time with for now.

She crossed her arms over her chest and gave him a critical glare. "Let me guess. You're Isaak Lee." When she smirked, the smile dropped from Isaak's face. "It all makes sense now."

"Excuse me? What makes sense?" How did she know who he was? And how much did she know about him? His odds of a casual conversation just plummeted like a plane with its engine bursting in flames on the way down.

"Why you'd need a tour guide for a minor camping trip." Dani cocked her head to the side. She sat down on the barstool behind the bar facing him.

"What is that supposed to mean? And where's Danny?" Isaak didn't like the way this conversation was going, not one bit.

"I'm Dani."

Isaak's jaw dropped for a split second before he recovered his witts. "I thought Danny was...."

She smirked again. "A man? You sound disappointed, Mr. Lee."

So much for taking the bull by the horns. He sighed. "Isaak, please. And I'm sorry. I just assumed that you were a male."

"You know what they say when you assume..."

Isaak gave her an awkward grin. "Yes, I do know. Please, can we just start over?" Isaak extended his hand to her. "I'm Isaak Lee, and you must be...."

After a moment's hesitation, Dani shook his hand. "Dani Skybird. So what brings you to Vancouver?"

"My editor thinks I need more exposure to the great outdoors." Which this woman clearly agreed with by the way she dressed him down so easily.

"I can see that." Dani nodded as she observed the way he was dressed. "You look like you've spent your life behind a desk."

"You know what they say," Isaak said, adjusting his tie, "don't ever judge a book by its cover."

"Unless the editor of that particular book has requested my help in getting some dirt under those nails." Dani nodded to his freshly manicured hands.

Isaak pulled his hands away self-consciously. Since when was hygiene unmanly? "Just because I'm a fan of personal hygiene doesn't mean I can't rough it in the woods with the best of them."

Dani raised a skeptical eyebrow at his statement. "We'll see about that. There'll be plenty to put your manhood to the test."

Isaak was sensing a challenge here. "Starting with?"

"We'll take a floatplane to the Bella Coola River, the Gateway to the Great Bear Rainforest. Then we'll make our way down the river before we head into the rainforest."

"Sounds easy enough." Not really, but Isaak was doing his damnedest to not let that thought be visible on his face.

The bartender carried a newly washed tray of glasses to the bar. Dani made the introduction. "Isaak, this is Jacob Skybird. He owns this place and the tour company."

Isaak shook hands with Jacob. "It's nice to meet you."

"You too."

"So, you're set to leave in the morning?" asked Jacob.

Isaak shrugged. "Sounds that way."

"You couldn't be in better hands." Jacob shared a secretive look with Dani.

"If I were you, I'd get plenty of rest, Mr. Lee," Dani said as she rose from the barstool. "Four-thirty is early for some, and it's going to be a long day tomorrow."

"It's Isaak, please, and I'm used to running marathons. A little stint in the forest isn't going to be a hardship."

Dani smirked, "We'll see."

"Yes, we will." Isaak tilted his glass and drained the rest of the beer. As he tossed his money on the bar, he got to his feet. "It was nice meeting you both. I'll be ready, bright and early."

Isaak turned to leave and had nearly made it to the door when Dani spoke. "Hey, city slicker…."

He cringed. City slicker? What century was this? This was going to be a long trip. Keep your cool, Isaak, my man. Remember you need her. He turned. "Yes?"

Her grin grew. "Make sure you wear something a little less dainty, will ya?"

Isaak looked down at his nicely pressed dress pants and white button-down shirt. There was nothing wrong with his clothes. Or at least he didn't think so until several patrons in the back of the bar laughed. He glanced at the laughing men, then back at Dani. Somehow he knew this was a test, and he'd better pass. "Don't worry. I came prepared."

Dani raised a skeptical eyebrow. "If you say so."

Isaak nodded, then turned and left with what remained of his dignity. "This job better be worth it," he said as the door closed behind him.

Chapter 4

Dani watched Isaak leave the bar and sighed. This was going to be a long trip, and she was not looking forward to it. Another ego maniacal male she would be forced to put in his place the whole time. Dani had dealt with plenty of those over the years. Most of them came here thinking that she was incapable of taking care of herself in the wilderness. The joke was on them, though. Dani had spent most of her time in the forest since she was a small child. Her father had made sure of it.

Dani looked over at Jacob Skybird and watched him staring at the door. The old man knew she could take care of herself, but still, he was protective, which was understandable, seeing as he was the man who had raised her. Some children grew up and flew the coop, but not Dani. The ties to her family and the land of her ancestors were too strong to ignore. There may have been a time she might have left, but that was before her mother had passed. Leaving her father alone was simply something she refused to do, especially now that he was sick.

Cancer. It was a six-letter word, nastier than any of the four-letter ones she'd ever learned. It was at the top of her list at the moment. Non-Hodgkins lymphoma, to be precise. Her father was doing well with his treatments and was no longer in the worst stage of the disease. His treatments had gone fairly smoothly, but even so, nothing in this life was guaranteed, and while he had several loyal employees ready to pick up the slack here, Dani was his right hand.

"Do me a favor. Don't go easy on him." Jacob nodded to the door with a gruff shake of his head.

Dani smiled at the comment. Going easy on Isaak was the last thing to cross her mind. She had plenty of things up her sleeve, and seeing how green Isaak was the moment he stepped into the bar would make all her plans easy to implement. This was going to be a very educational trip for that city slicker, and she would find some entertainment from it too. It had been a while since she had dressed down a shirt and tie. The suits were always the best to take through the woods, especially when they came with their brand new pristine boots. That reminded her that she should pack more Band-Aids. Blisters were a sure bet if he didn't have the forethought to break them in ahead of time. Dani wondered how delicate Isaak really was. On a scale of one to ten, she'd rank him at an eight, maybe a nine. Especially going off of what his boss had told her. That woman was a riot and a half. Dani almost wished the woman was coming in his place.

Dani placed her hand on Jacob's arm. "Don't worry, I don't plan on it."

Jacob smiled at his daughter and nodded his head. "That's my girl." It was like he could see all the plans floating around in her head. Half of them he had planted in there over her lifetime. How to keep the outsiders on the outside and refuse to let them really in. Jacob was a professional, where shutting people out was concerned. Even his relationship with his wife had been slightly stilted. The only person who had ever come close to understanding him was Dani. They were two peas in a pod.

"Give 'em hell, right?" Dani shrugged.

"You sure you're all right, Dani?" Her father was anything if astute.

"I'm fine, don't worry." She pushed his words away. They were thoughts she didn't want to conjure up right now. The cautionary tale that she would always have to remind herself, even though it had been at least a year since her world had fallen out from under her.

"He looks a little…."

"Like Jason? Not really," she lied. Isaak was the same height and build as her former love, even the same skin tone, but his eyes were different. Where Jason's had been dark chocolate, Isaak's were lighter and seemed to change as the light hit them. Not that Dani was checking him out, she was simply used to taking in the details of all her surroundings, including the people that were planted inside them.

"That man better hope I never catch him this side of the world any time soon," grumbled Jacob.

"Don't worry. He had bigger plans than setting up shop anywhere near here," Dani placated her father. The truth was that Dani had no idea where Jason had ended up. Only that she didn't mean enough to him for him to settle down around here. They had been together for a few years, and while he had grown up around here, Jason had always had the bright lights of the city tattooed in his mind. Some days it was all the man thought about. Not Dani. She would be damned if she would be stuck in a concrete jungle, where the only mountains visible were the high-rise buildings.

Oddly enough, it wasn't their differences that had ended their relationship. No, it was Jason's lack of empathy for what her father was going through at the time. Jason had demanded more and more of her time at a time when her father really needed her. Dani refused to abandon her father in his hour of need, and Jason had retaliated like some toddler being refused his favorite cookie. In a way, Dani was relieved he had shown all his colors before they had done something more permanent, like get married and have children. She shivered at the thought of raising pretentious children with that man. Even though she would have wanted them to know their roots, Jason would have done everything he could to keep their roots buried in the past.

Men! Why did they always think their hopes and dreams were what made the world go round? Where would a man be without the strong back of the woman behind him? While her parents hadn't been openly romantic in their relationship, there was nothing her parents wouldn't have done for each other. Her mother had always put the Blue Moon first, helping to get the bar off the ground when her father had purchased it so long ago. Mom had created the first menu. Some of her recipes were still a favorite for the regulars. Iris had been firm in her support and gentle in her encouragement when the numbers looked bad.

Sometimes Dani wondered if her mother had a dream of her own that she had given up on. Iris had always seemed content to support those around her. Dani didn't think she was capable of doing that herself. Then again, Dani was living her dream. A small cabin overlooking the world below, a foot in the future, but one in the past as she kept it firmly planted in the land of her ancestors. Dani felt like she had the best of every world right here under the aurora sky.

Dani shook her thoughts away. The time to wander through them was not at hand. There was plenty of work to be done here before she took off on her trip in the morning. She had a feeling she would need all the energy she could get. More than likely, Dani would have to pull more than her own weight because Isaak looked like he had never even taken a walk off the beaten path before, much less experience any of the things she was about to show him. "Well, I better finish up here. Do you need me to close?"

"Nah. I got it. Go get some rest. I have a feeling that one's going to give you a run for your money." Jacob smiled at Dani.

"You're probably right. But it's nothing I can't handle." Even if he did look like Jason. Dani would make sure to keep her memories separate from the present; otherwise, she would be holding Isaak accountable for someone else's actions. Dani would have to compartmentalize this trip. That was going to be tons of fun, more like brushing her teeth with a scouring pad. She didn't know which one would be more pleasant. All she knew was she couldn't afford to pass up the work. These trips were few and far between lately. With the tourism industry selling coastal cruises in lieu of outdoor experiences, it was getting harder and harder to get a tour group going. This article that the outdoor magazine would put out could bring a little more tourism to their area. It could be good for the whole area, not just her guided tours.

All she had to do was make sure Isaak had a trip he never forgot. And keep him safe from his own ineptitude. That was probably going to be easier said than done. Nevertheless, she was the perfect guide for the task. Knocking the chip off his shoulder was the first thing on the agenda. He might not realize he carried it there, but Dani could see it the minute she stepped up to the bar. City boys. They were always a handful, but Dani had always managed them just fine. This trip would be no different.

Chapter 5

Four in the morning came awfully early for Isaak, and the feeling of jetlag didn't help either. When the alarm on his phone pealed loudly, he nearly tossed it across the room. Contrary to what he implied the night before to Dani, he was not an early morning person. Never had been and never would be.

This trip was already his least favorite. The fact that he had to test his mettle in front of a woman didn't make him feel any better, especially considering how attractive said woman was. No man ever wanted to make a fool of himself in front of a woman like Dani.

Dani, what an unusual name for a girl. He wondered if it was short for Danielle or something else like that. Isaak certainly didn't expect his guide to be a female. He probably should have asked for more details from Angel. She did seem rather smug when she informed him of this assignment. Angel was probably having a field day, knowing that not only would Isaak be traipsing off into the woods for the first time in his life, but he would be doing it under the purview of a woman who would probably be laughing at him the entire time. Isaak didn't think he was a chauvinist, but the idea that he would be taking instructions from a woman made him feel just a tad weaker than he already did.

Then again, how would he feel if he had to pretend to be even more macho in front of some caveman? That wasn't a fair assessment of an outdoorsman, though, was it? Just because they had skills he didn't, that didn't mean Isaak should be blasting them with his own judgments. The fact that he didn't go fishing or chop his own wood didn't make someone who did a neanderthal.

Beep! Beep! Beep! "Dammit." Isaak glared at the phone, which was giving another warning peal. No time for these ridiculous thoughts. They wouldn't help him anyway. The only thing he needed right now was a gallon of strong coffee so he could keep his wits about him because, let's face it, his sense of humor and wit would be the only thing that would get him out of this in one piece. He didn't particularly care to make a fool out of himself, but he would survive it, and hopefully, his experiences would give him enough to write a decent article. Would it be Pulitzer Prize worthy? Probably not, but it would help him keep his job until the dust settled. One day soon, he'd be able to get back to the world of journalism. For now, he had to keep his feet wet wherever he could.

Isaak quickly got ready for the day, well, as fast as his body would move on so little sleep. He needed caffeine and lots of it. Isaak put on the new clothes he had purchased for the trip: jeans, a t-shirt and a flannel button-up overshirt, warm socks, and the new boots the clerk had told him were the best for hiking. The boots were loud and clunky and made him feel a little like a clown as he walked down the hallway from his room, but he would get over that eventually. He'd just pretend they were hightops from back in the day and forget the stiff edge that seemed to rub a little tight against the back of his heel. He was sure that would change after wearing them for a little while.

He met Dani outside in the parking lot. The sun hadn't yet risen on the horizon, and the woman had the audacity to look bright and shiny way too early. She might be a morning person, but he sure as hell wasn't. He nodded at her in greeting.

"Ready, Isaak?" she asked him.

"As ready as I'm going to be," he half mumbled.

"What's the matter? Not used to daybreak?" Dani smirked at him. "Don't worry. We still have a little trip before we start our day. You can catch a cat nap."

A nap. He could go for that right now. It sounded like heaven. Isaak almost gave her a relieved smile but stopped himself. He didn't want to confirm her suspicions, nor was he prepared to look like a lightweight. "I'm good."

"Uh-huh. We'll drive to the dock and catch a seaplane to the Bella Coola River, right in the heart of the Great Bear Rainforest. These are our packs for the trip. I packed one for you, just in case."

"Okay. Let's do this." Isaak picked up one of the

packs at Dani's feet and tried not to look too relieved. He had a few things in his own bag, but by the size of the packs at her feet, he had severely under-packed. Following Dani to her car, he helped load the packs into the trunk, then joined her in the front seat.

He wasn't sure if he should be happy that she said very little to him while they drove to the meetup place. It was probably wise to start out slow with the conversational topics. They would be stuck with each other for several days, and that proximity could get aggravating really fast, especially if she treated him like a 'city slicker' the whole time. Isaak resolved himself to staring out the window and pretending not to have a care in the world as Dani drove them to the docks.

As the car pulled into the parking lot, Isaak could see the floatplane near the end of the dock. He had never been on a floatplane before and was actually intrigued by the prospect. He cataloged the setting in his mind, so he could write the scene later. The red and white plane floated on two pontoons, allowing it to land on the water and skim over the water as it prepared to take off. His only experience with planes and water was praying the one he was aboard didn't decide to take a nose dive into the ocean. The floatplane was practically made for it. Maybe that was why his heartbeat was just a little faster as Dani put the car in park.

He could see the pilot from here. The man looked to be in his mid-forties. He was standing outside of the floatplane, waiting for their arrival. When the pilot saw Dani step out of the car, he waved at her. Dani gave him a genuine smile and waved back. Isaak was surprised by it, for everything he had noticed about her so far was her wit and the way she dressed him down. He had a feeling she didn't like outsiders at all. His suspicions were confirmed only seconds later.

Dani turned around and gave him an irritated glance. "Are you coming? Or did you decide to pack it in already?"

Was it him that she specifically didn't like, or was it, men, in general? This was going to be a long trip. Isaak counted to three in his head before he responded. "I'll get the bags."

Dani didn't even turn to him as she started for the floatplane. Isaak watched her as he retrieved the backpacks from the trunk. It seemed like the two of them knew each other pretty well because the moment Dani stepped up to the plane, she and the pilot engaged in conversation.

Isaak tried not to be offended when the man said very little to him. To the pilot, Isaak was nothing more than a passenger. Besides reassuring him that they would be safe in the air, that was all there was to it. At least the man helped him store the backpacks in the compartments of the pontoons.

As they flew over the Bella Coola river, Isaak remained aloof. He listened as Dani pointed out key features of the river from the sky and gave the obligatory nod here and there, but he kept his thoughts to himself, mostly because he was still trying to get his brain to wake up.

Isaak could see how the area could attract many people. It was a beautiful place with breathtaking views of the surrounding landscapes and waterways. As the floatplane soared closer to the Great Bear Rainforest, he could see the densely packed trees and foliage covering the ground below. It was expansive, and it suddenly hit him that he would be trapped inside it with a guide who had already written him off as some lightweight city slicker. To be honest, she wasn't far from the truth with that but damned if he'd let her know that.

The floatplane turned and headed toward the river lining the coast. As he gazed down at the water, he could see the sun shimmering on the small waves. He hated to admit it, but the view was spectacular and somehow peaceful. He wondered what it would be like to wake up to this view every day. Before he could finish that thought, the plane was descending to its destination. Landing was always the worst part. Isaak braced himself for the touchdown.

"You ready for this?" Dani asked him with a smirk on her face.

Isaak glanced at Dani, noting her expression, then brought his attention back to the scenery outside the window. On the shore, near the river, were several racks of kayaks and a locked box containing life jackets. Just what exactly was he supposed to be ready for? He turned to Dani and refused to let her see any weak link in his confidence. "Born ready."

To Isaak's relief, the plane touched down without a hitch. As they exited the plane, the pilot was already outside on the dock. He was placing the backpacks on the wooden planks near the plane's steps. Extending his hand, he helped Dani step off the plane.

"Thank you, Roger."

"Of course," the pilot answered.

Roger held his hand out to assist Isaac, but Isaac waved the hand away. Roger pulled his hand back and stepped away from the plane. "Suit yourself."

Dani turned around to address the pilot. "Don't take it personally. You know how macho some men get."

Roger chuckled at her remark. "Oh, believe me, I don't. We get a lotta city folk this time of year. Most have that macho attitude, to begin with. By the time I come back to pick them up, attitudes change."

"Macho? I'm not macho." What a ridiculous thing for her and the pilot both to assume, just because he was city-born and raised. Isaak tried to brush it off and not let their words get to him. As he started down the small steps, he ended up smacking the top of his head on the door frame. Of course, he did. Why not? The odds were ever in his favor, apparently. He saw Dani turn her head away quickly as she hid her amusement. This was going to be the trip from hell.

Guaranteed.

"Watch out for your head. The first step's a doozy," the humor in Roger's voice was easy to hear.

Isaak glared at the grinning pilot. "Thanks for the warning." He resisted the urge to rub the tender spot now throbbing on his scalp. His pride wouldn't let him.

Isaak picked up the backpack Dani had packed for him and walked away from the plane, not bothering to see if Dani followed him or not. He assumed they would start their adventure by using the kayaks tied up on the stand. Isaak had never been in a kayak in his life. With the way his luck was going, he'd capsize the thing and drown while she sat there laughing at him.

Why should he care, though? He had never done this before. Did caring about what she thought make him macho? Would he worry as much if it were a male escorting him on this trip? With a man, he'd shoot the breeze, laugh off his mistakes and pretend he meant to do anything that made him look ridiculous. It was some sort of bro code. Why did men feel the need to be stronger and bolder when the opposite sex was involved? It's not like they were back in caveman days, where he was expected to smack her over the head with a club and carry her away. Even if they were, Dani would probably beat him to it. He would find his ass being carted away into the bush long before he ever got the drop on her. She was a wild card.

While he stood there, waiting for Dani, he watched her talking to the pilot. The two were sharing some serious moment. Maybe they were discussing trip details. Turning away from them, he decided to take in the surrounding area. Isaak pulled out his cell phone and started to take photos of the sun on the river. He wanted to remember little details, and maybe taking pictures of them would be the easiest way to jog his memory. He panned around, taking different photos. He was so focused on his pictures that he never heard Dani walk up to him.

"Whatcha looking at?"

His heart skipped a couple of beats. "Crap." Isaak jumped and nearly dropped his phone. It slipped through his fingers, and Dani caught it midair with ninja-like skills.

"Careful." She handed the phone over to Isaak.

"Do you have to sneak up on people?" Isaak

accused her.

Dani gave him a teasing smile. "Would you rather I stomp around like an elephant?"

"No, I suppose that wouldn't be a good idea out in the wild." Isaak caught the floatplane taking off in the corner of his eye and turned to take a quick picture of the plane.

Dani stepped over to the stand holding the kayaks. Untying one of the kayaks on the bottom, she started to drag it out. "Help me with this, will you?"

"Of course." Isaak moved closer and grabbed one of the ends.

As they balanced the kayak between them, Dani motioned toward the shore with a nod of her head. "Over there."

"Sure." Isaak helped her carry it to the water's edge and lower it to the ground. The kayak was still far enough on the land that it wouldn't take off in the water by itself.

"One more?" asked Isaak. He was prepared for the quiet nod of her reply. It made sense because these were traditional kayaks that only held one person. They both headed back to the rack.

Dani gave him a once over as they stood there. "This is a far reach, but here goes. You've done this before, right?"

Isaak snorted loudly. "Afraid not."

As they grabbed the next kayak, Dani sighed to herself. "I guess there'll be a lot of firsts on this trip then. It's kinda like riding a bike."

As they walked the kayak to the other one, Isaak chuckled to himself. "Let me guess. Make a mistake, and it'll hurt like hell?"

Dani nodded. "I was going to say once you learn, you never forget, but I like your response. Yep, that 'bout covers it."

Dani dusted off her hands and pointed to Isaak's kayak. "Start securing your backpack to the straps on the back while I lock the kayak stand. Be sure to secure it tight. Everything you'll need for the duration of this trip is in that bag. If you lose it...."

"Got it. Don't lose the supplies," interrupted Isaak. He looked down at his phone and saw the lack of bars.

Dani noticed. "Yeah, you won't have service out here. No cell towers."

"Great. So we're definitely roughing then." Isaak sighed as he shoved his phone into this backpack and dug out his camera instead. He held up the camera before looping the strap behind his neck. "Hopefully, I brought enough batteries to last the trip."

Dani chuckled. "Hope so. No charging stations, either."

Isaak watched as Dani locked the kayak rack, grabbed two life jackets and made her way back to him. Isaak started to tie the backpack to the back of his kayak, hoping that he had done enough to keep it in place. He stood up and made sure his camera was strapped securely around his neck.

As he did, Dani came over to inspect his work. She leaned down and made one simple tug. Just one and all his work came unraveled. The backpack fell off the back of his kayak.

He was dumbfounded. "Hey!" Isaak complained.

"Ya gotta do better than that. I don't want to spend half a day chasing your supplies up the river." Dani knelt down and showed Isaak how to do it properly as she secured her own backpack to her kayak. "Like this."

"Show off," grumbled Isaak as he attempted to secure his backpack in the way Dani demonstrated. When he was done, he could see the difference. Part of him wanted to show it off, like a kindergartener showing his first art project off to his teacher. That made him feel even less manly. Instead, he kept quiet and waited for his next instructions. He didn't have to wait long.

Dani handed Isaak a life jacket. "Put this on. We're burning daylight."

A woman of few words, who knew? Isaak put on the life jacket and followed everything Dani did next. Before he knew it, he was inside his kayak on the river. Initially, paddling was awkward as he twisted his body from side to side to get the right rhythm, but before long, he was able to keep up the Dani.

Chapter 6

It was not a normal day for Dani. She would much rather be heading down the Bella Coola River in a kayak on a solitary journey. She'd done that enough in her lifetime to almost travel it blindfolded. As far as travel companions went, she'd had worse than Isaak, not that she would tell him that anytime soon. He was actually catching on faster than she thought he would, even though he nearly toppled over three times already. Nearly, that was the keyword. Somehow, he managed to straighten himself out before that happened.

Dani reached over and scooped loose strands of kelp up with her oar. She laid it across the front of the kayak to use later. Angel had asked for the full outdoor survival experience, and that meant showing Isaak how to survive off what nature provided for them. Kelp was one of the things she used as a meal replacement. Add in some nuts and berries over a fire, and she had a delicious meal. The question was, how would Isaak like it? She'd had a handful of people turn their noses up completely. Eventually, hunger would set in, though, and they would give in, whether they wanted to or not. It was much easier to feed the willing than someone against trying new things.

Dani held her hand up to her forehead to block the sun from her eyes as she scanned the area around them. The sun was high in the sky, and its heat was magnified by the lapping waves they sluiced through. From the river, she could see the deep forests that she knew so well. Dani had spent most of her life exploring every inch of the Great Bear Rainforest. Even the snow-topped mountains towering above the trees were calling her name. Come, Dani. Home.

Home. Where the gentle breeze could turn to a whipping wind at any point in time. This world of hers was alive and free, just like her. She smiled at the fish that flopped out of the water nearby. The loud plop distracted her from her thoughts, and she reminded herself to keep focused. They had more distance to cover.

Behind her, she heard Isaak snapping pictures with his camera. He was a man of few words. Something they actually had in common, but she doubted he was nearly as introspective as she was. When Dani looked out at the world surrounding them, she saw all the infinite possibilities around her. The life force of the water as it brought sustenance to the lands, the huge oxygenators in the forest, and the many wondrous creatures that bustled around the area from one place to the next. For instance, the grizzly bear cubs nearly hidden from view on the tree line. The cubs were wrestling each other without a care in the world. Oh, to live in that simplistic world before the corruption of others stepped in and ruined it.

Dani had been working with the area rangers to protect the bears in the Great Bear Rainforest. Hunting inside the rainforest was illegal, but that didn't stop people from breaking the rules. She'd often helped bears that had been downed by hunters that were often hunting the bears just for sport. Some would hunt them for trophies. It was a disgusting situation.

She tried to push those thoughts away. This was not the time to dwell. Dani needed to keep her senses about her. She was responsible for Isaak's safety, after all. While the forest may seem peaceful to everyone else, she knew there were dangers around them. It was her job to be aware of them.

More time passed as they rowed along in silence. The occasional click of the camera could be heard behind her. At least he was capturing some of nature's splendor. The sun had moved, and now the trees were casting long shadows. Tall, sheer cliffs towered on both sides of the river. As they continued along, the shoreline opened up to a place to anchor the boats and stop for the night.

Dani pointed to the shore and called out to Isaak. "We'll camp here tonight."

"Good! I'm starving." Isaak was eager to follow her.

After pulling the kayaks to shore, Dani packed the now-dried kelp in her bag, and they spent the next hour setting up the camp. They had cleared a small area and gathered wood to make a fire in the middle.

Well, Dani had. She had a better eye for dry wood than Isaak, but she gave him a few pointers that he seemed to file away somewhere in his head.

The sun set quickly, and it was a clear night. The sky was full of stars, and only the sound of the crackling fire and chirping crickets punctuated the silence. Their sleeping bags were laid out across from the fire. Dani made sure to put proper distance between them. She didn't want him getting any ideas. Not that he would. Isaak seemed to be more of a gentleman than she first assumed. He responded politely to her and smiled when she gave him pointers. It was a little unnerving, really. Dani had expected him to be a real hard ass. That's what the city folk usually did on these excursions, and when it was anyone from the male persuasion, pigheadedness was something that ran rampant. Isaak didn't match her preconceived notion.

Isaak smiled, clapped his hands together and rubbed them in anticipation. "What's for dinner?"

Dani tossed him an apple from her pack. "Here."

Isaak looked at the apple, failing to hide the disappointment. Dani laughed and pulled out a cloth bundle. She reached over and handed it to him. "Enjoy it while you can."

Isaak sat down on his sleeping bag and started to unwrap his bundle but looked up at Dani suspiciously. "Why?"

Dani opened her own bundle that contained two sandwiches and a protein bar. "This is the only meal provided on this journey. Other than some protein bars, jerky, and hardtack, this is it."

Isaak's expression went slack with confusion. "One meal, that's absurd. This trip is supposed to be ten days. There's no way two sandwiches and some fruit will be enough to sustain us for ten days. I don't understand." Isaak stared at her in disbelief. "What kind of a touring company are you running here?"

Dani smirked at him. "Our company is top-notch for one-on-one private tours. Your editor was very specific. She insisted you have the full nature experience. That's what you're getting."

"But...." Isaak looked as if he were searching for words.

"Don't worry. I will be teaching you to be self-sufficient, and you'll learn to live off what nature provides you. I won't let you starve, Isaak...much."

Isaak glared at his sandwich and grumbled under his breath. "Angel will be hearing a few choice words from me when I get back."

Dani tried to hide the smile that was forming on her face. She found his situation more than just a little amusing. He looked like a petulant child right now. She couldn't help poking the bear, so to speak. "If you don't think you can handle it, Mr. Lee. I can use the satellite phone and call the pilot back out. I can have you back in Vancouver in two days."

Isaak turned back quickly in disbelief. His jaw hung slack. "Two days? It only took us six hours or so to get here."

"We would have to hike back by foot through the forest. The current isn't in our favor to take the kayaks back in the other direction." Dani paused to let her words take effect. "So, what will it be, Isaak? Do I need to call the pilot?"

Isaak sighed loudly before he hung his head in defeat. "No. I need this job. I need to prove myself to a lot of people."

Dani almost felt sorry for him. He was speaking from the heart, whether he knew it or not. There was a desperation inside him that Dani almost understood. The need to prove himself. She had been just as driven to prove herself in a man's world. Her father had raised her to be strong and independent. What had he been raised to be? Breadwinner? Did he have a family to support somewhere? She hadn't seen a ring on his finger, but not all married men wore them. Why was she even having thoughts about that?

"Good choice. You'll need to finish eating and get some rest. We have a long day ahead of us tomorrow."

Dani watched Isaak as he stared into the fire while eating the last few bites of the sandwich. She noticed a determined resolve in his posture. She had to give him credit. He was trying.

Dani looked up at the sky and wondered how long it would take her to fall asleep tonight. She was usually keyed up when she slept under the open sky. When her body soaked up the energy swirling around her, she was rejuvenated. The world was filled with endless possibilities, from the gentle hum of the earth below her to the brilliant glow in the sky. That was what she loved most about being so attuned to nature.

"Good night," Isaak called to her as he slid into

his sleeping bag.

"Night," was her reply. She climbed into her bag and tried to get some sleep as well.

As the hours passed, Dani tossed and turned inside her bag. Isaak was snoring like a fog horn leading a stranded ship to the shore. How could anyone sleep that deeply in unfamiliar territory? She was half tempted to chuck a rock at his head, but that would probably result in homicide. That would certainly stain her travel guide record, not to mention she'd find herself trapped inside four walls and never see this beautiful world again. Instead, she lay there staring at the stars, wondering how the hell she was going to make it through the next few days.

Somehow, she forged through until dawn, catching just enough sleep to function. Dani wouldn't let a bad night's sleep keep her from starting her day. There was too much to be done if they were going to stay on track and reach their destination on time. The first light of dawn was just now pushing its way through the clouds to the ground below. Dani started rolling up her sleeping bag next to the campfire that had fizzled out during the night.

Isaak started to wake up slowly. He turned over and squinted at her. "Do you have to be so loud?"

Dani snorted in disbelief. "Me? You snore louder than a bear in hibernation."

"I don't snore," grumbled Isaak.

Dani rolled her eyes and continued packing. So, he was a grumpy bear in the morning. She should have known better than to expect a quiet morning. So far, he hadn't been too intolerable, but her nerves were already frayed from having less than the normal amount of sleep.

Isaak sat up and stretched. His body was visibly sore from sleeping on the ground and a day of rowing as his body twinged slightly as he moved it. "Does it get any easier?"

"What?" asked Dani.

Isaak nodded to the ground under him. "The ground feels like concrete."

Dani shook her head. "Well, it's not the Four Seasons. What did you expect?"

Isaak looked down at the bag he had just started rolling up. "Someone isn't a morning person."

Dani scowled at him but didn't say another word

as she wrapped the tie around her sleeping bag. She was afraid if she opened her mouth, all the things she had been thinking all night long would come flying out like some vicious diarrhea of the mouth. She wouldn't be able to take any of that back. Instead, she tossed him a granola bar. "Here."

Isaak grinned at her. "Now, this is what I call a continental breakfast."

Dani's face relaxed when she realized he was only teasing her. Maybe she was taking this a little too seriously right now. "If you think this is good, wait until you see what I have planned for lunch."

"Please tell me you're not going to feed me bark." A flush of panic filled his face.

Dani clucked her tongue behind her teeth to tisk at him. "Don't knock it 'til you've tried it."

Isaak finished the rest of his bar and shoved the wrapper into his pack. He murmured to himself, "Remind me to kill Angel."

Dani turned to look at him. "What's that?"

Isaak looked up at her and shrugged. "Nothing."

Dani had to keep things moving. They had a schedule to keep to. "Be ready in ten."

"Minutes?" Isaak had an incredulous look on his face.

Dani smirked at him. She couldn't resist one last hit. "What? Not enough time to powder your face?"

Isaak shook his head at her, clearly holding back a comment. "Don't worry, I'll be ready in seven."

Chapter 7

Now that they were packed up and ready to go, the two of them stood next to each other. Isaak could tell that Dani was hanging by a thread. She reminded him of a woman who was very much in need of a coffee or a fancy mocha latte or some caffeinated beverage alternative. He wouldn't mind having some himself. Last night he had zonked out the minute his head hit the ground, and while he had slept through the night, it wasn't the best night's sleep he had ever had. All his joints and muscles already ached, and he hadn't even started out for the day. He'd just have to suck it up.

Isaak rolled his shoulders to dislodge the kink. It didn't work. It was going to be a long day. He could feel it. "So where to?"

"We're heading into the rainforest this morning," answered Dani.

Isaak looked at the boats on the shore. "What? We just leave them here?"

Dani turned to look at the kayaks, then back at Isaak. "Yes. We work with a company that will retrieve them for us. We'll be on foot for the duration."

That's just great. Isaak didn't mind a walk here or there, but he hadn't realized Angel had signed him up for cross-country hiking. Isaak had to keep his cool, no matter how much he wanted to throw an adult tantrum right now. He'd just have to trek through the woods and pretend that nothing was the matter, even though every muscle in his body was already planning a full-on rebellion this morning. "Alrighty then."

Isaak watched Dani walk away. He picked up his camera and snapped a few pictures. Turning the lens toward Dani, he caught a picture of her, with sunlight illuminating her face. The simple beauty around her only enhanced her own charm. Even though she appeared to be quite the cynic, Isaak found himself intrigued by her. Snapping a few more pictures, he turned his camera in another direction when she turned around to look at him.

"Ready to move?" she asked him.

"Born ready." Isaak ignored the derisive snort she tried to hide. He reminded himself that his mother didn't raise him to be so damned thinned-skinned. It was time to push his little complaints aside and put his best foot forward, even if it killed him, and at this rate, it just might.

Isaak followed Dani up the shore, taking more candid shots here and there. She turned around to face him when he took another picture of her.

"Do you mind?" Dani looked like she was ready to snatch the camera out of his hands.

Isaak held back a grin. She was a feisty one. "Afraid to have your picture taken?"

She held his gaze. "No. But it's a courtesy to ask first."

"Don't worry, I won't publish it." He quickly changed the subject when she looked like she would object further. "So, tell me more about the Great Bear Rainforest."

"What do you want to know?"

Since he didn't know anything about it, Isaak could stand to learn as much as possible. "Everything."

Dani looked thoughtful for a moment. "It's one of the largest temperate rainforests in the world, protected by the sanctions that keep it safe from destruction."

Isaak continued snapping photos as they started to enter the rainforest. He spied a raven overhead. The bird cawed at him when he zeroed in on it. The bird seemed to glare at him when he snapped its picture. "Guess he doesn't like his picture taken either."

The bird yelled at him again before taking flight. When it landed on a branch closer to him, Isaak barely avoided the bird poop aimed his way. Isaak jumped back as the bird continued to glare and appeared to be restocking his defecating arsenal as his feathers puffed up around him.

"Disgusting. Shoo! Get!!" Isaak stepped closer to the tree and flapped his hand upward to shoo the raven away.

Dani leaned back against a tree and studied Isaak and the bird. "You look like an idiot, you know that?" She shook her head and sighed.

Isaak was incredulous. "Me? That bird seems to

have a problem with me."

"The only thing he is guilty of is his poor aim," teased Dani.

Isaak saw the small smile slide across her lips. Her face seemed softer the moment she did. "I see how you are. Let's see how you feel when he targets you."

"He wouldn't." Dani's voice was confident.

"Why so sure?"

"Because I see him for what he really is." Dani's eyes held a far-off gaze.

"What? A filthy blackbird?" suggested Isaak. He hadn't seen too many of them in the city. Pigeons were more common there, and those birds were filled with disgusting diseases. Isaak imagined the same was true for these birds.

Dani glared at Isaak. "That is a raven. And its lineage is much greater than any of yours. He is a symbol to many people. For him to show himself is an honor."

Isaak muttered under his breath, "Until he marks you."

Dani ignored him and started to move forward again.

Isaak could tell his remark had hit a nerve. It was just a bird. What was the big deal, anyway? He grinned as he thought of all the things he could have said to stir the pot further. Then again, he didn't want her to desert him in the middle of the Great Bear Rainforest. He probably only had four more granola bars in his backpack. Today, they would be roughing it, and that wasn't something he was looking forward to, but if he could survive the school lunch pizza, he could eat almost anything.

Isaak followed her in silence, keeping his thoughts on lockdown. His brain was full of them. Even here, he couldn't shut down the thoughts that seemed to cycle inside them like a street courier. As the trail started to shift. The terrain changed from just dirt and trees to now include rocks of various sizes. Isaak was looking everywhere at once, taking pictures and continuing to walk without paying attention to the road ahead. He never saw Dani pause in her tracks, a fact that was easy to see as he plowed straight into her, managing to knock both of them to the ground in the process.

Dani groaned slightly and rubbed her backside

as she glared at him. "Pay attention, will you?"

Isaak picked himself up off the ground and extended his hand to her, which she ignored completely. "Sorry. I was a little distracted."

"If you let little distractions get to you out here, you'll miss the things you're meant to see," cautioned Dani.

"Like what?"

Dani reached up to put her hands on his face. She jerked his head toward the rocks near them. On these rocks were symbols that had been carved over time. "Nature is more than just taking a walk. These are petroglyphs. They're filled with the history of everything that came before and everything that will come after. It's why many people find refuge in the woods."

He raised his camera and snapped a picture before he turned to her again. "Like my readers?" asked Isaak with interest.

"I suppose." Danni shrugged. "I've never had to read about being in the wild, though. I've always lived it."

Isaak tried to figure out whether she was taking

another shot at him. "I guess we're not all so lucky."

Dani sighed. "No, we're not."

Moving closer to the stone carvings, he took more photos that showed the contrast between the grey rock and green moss. He was intrigued by the history in front of him. Never in a million years would he have thought to find something like that out in the middle of the wilderness. This little piece made him feel a little more connected to the world that came before him. Is that what it felt like to commune with mother nature? To enjoy the great outdoors instead of the concrete jungle he lived in? "It's almost like they tell a story." Isaak ran his fingers over the carving.

"They do. They tell everything and nothing."

Isaak snorted softly. "Always so cryptic."

"I'm not cryptic. Just reflective. Perhaps you should learn to be the same." Dani stepped away from him and studied the ground nearby.

Isaak put a little distance between them as he walked between a few trees. He was still not watching where he was walking at all. "Reflective...I'll show you reflective."

As he continued to walk, he nearly stepped on

what he thought was a stick. That first glance was definitely playing a trick on him, for when he looked closer, it was clear that the stick was not a stick at all. A snake was winding its way across the dirt floor of the forest. It was moving away from Isaak, but that didn't seem to register in his brain. All he saw was a snake, and his body went into full panic mode. He jumped back and tried not to shriek like a little girl. "What the...."

Dani laughed at his panic. "Relax. It's just a common garter snake. More afraid of you than you'll ever be of it."

"You sure about that? That thing had fangs the size of an ice pick." Isaak held up his hand as if to demonstrate how large the fangs were.

Dani shook her head at him while he grinned at her. "You're such a lightweight. Don't worry. I'll let you know when there's something to worry about."

Isaak's eyebrows rose curiously. "Like what?"

Dani pursed her lips together thoughtfully as if trying to measure her reply. "You don't want to know." She glanced around the surrounding area before returning her gaze to Isaak. "Let's keep moving.

There's more ground to cover."

Dani was already moving on, but Isaak wasn't quite ready to move yet. His heart was still racing a little faster than he cared to admit, and her lack of an explanation hadn't left him reassured either. What other terrors might be lurking in these woods? Isaak mentally shook himself. Don't go there. Just one foot in front of the other, Isaak. The snake is gone. Nothing to see here, right? He took one tentative step and nearby jumped out of his skin for the second time as a nut came crashing down from the tree above him. It landed at his feet but was still too close for comfort. Isaak looked up at the tree and saw the raven sitting on one of the branches.

"You again? I see your aim hasn't improved." Isaak held his chin up at the bird as if raising a challenge. The bird tilted its head and stared him down before crowing at him again. "Fine, I'm moving. Just keep your feathers on, will ya?"

Chapter 8

As they continued on, the sun was high in the sky. Its rays were shining brightly through the trees, and while there was plenty of shade, the forest around them was starting to heat up a bit. Dani could see the sweat pouring down Isaak's face. She was surprised that he hadn't started complaining. Most city slickers would be begging for a break by now, especially since it was well past lunchtime. Not Isaak. He was a man of few words, well, unless he was dodging projectiles from overhead or shrieking at garter snakes.

Dani could still see him jumping out of his gourd. She wanted to laugh every time she thought about it. That was a priceless moment. Funny enough, though, that wasn't the first time she had seen a grown man jump at the sight of a snake. Sometimes they screamed at spiders too. She secretly hoped he walked into a web just to see how he'd react. It was a cruel thought, one she just couldn't seem to let go of.

Good thing he couldn't read her mind. If he could, Isaak would find out that she wasn't nearly as cold as she made herself out to be. Strangely enough, she found herself intrigued by him. He was not afraid to make fun of himself and make the best of the situation. She couldn't say the same about herself. If her job had made her go somewhere that sent her completely out of her element, Dani would have trouble finding the bright side of things. And if they sent her to the big city where she was just a number in the masses, that would probably make her lose her mind.

For the past few minutes, Dani had started showing Isaak the animal tracks that were nearly invisible to the rest of the world. She smiled when she saw him start to take pictures of them. At least the man was taking it seriously, maybe too seriously. He would need a new camera card soon, with the number of pictures he'd already taken. Now the tracks had stopped as the forest opened up to a small clearing.

Dani pressed on full speed ahead. The faster they reached their destination, the faster they could put food in their bellies. Having had very little sleep, trying to walk a marathon on an empty stomach wasn't a wise move. Dani had done it many times before, but she couldn't afford to push Isaak that hard. It wasn't like she would be able to carry him out of here. He was a good head taller than her, and even though she couldn't see the flesh beneath his clothes, she could tell he was in good shape.

Isaak stopped walking and called out to Dani in a winded voice. "Do you always walk for hours on end?"

Dani stopped walking and turned around to look at Isaak. She had been so focused on pushing forward that she hadn't realized that he had stopped walking. He did look a little pathetic, panting slightly as he leaned over to catch his breath. "I thought you ran marathons?"

Isaak managed a small grin. "I have. Maybe not so recently."

Dani smiled. "Thought so. Do you need a break?"

"If I say yes, will you think me less of a man?" His face turned serious.

Dani didn't like where this discussion was going. "Less? That would imply I think of you at all."

"Oh, come on. Admit it. I'm growing on you." His had a mischievous glow.

"Like a wart I can't get rid of." Dani smiled despite herself. Isaak returned the smile, and when he did, Dani felt something flip over in her stomach. No, no. None of those thoughts are allowed, girl. He's just a client you are taking through the forest. Once it's all said and done, he will return to where he came from. It really was uncanny how much he looked like Jason. His mannerisms were not far off either, although he wasn't faking interest in the world around them here. This was all new to him, and his eyes were wide open. She loved that she got to see that firsthand.

"Any chance you got any more food in that pack?"

"Just some hardtack," answered Dani.

Isaak shuddered. "Well, that sounds appetizing. Wish we could have brought more fresh food."

"Don't worry. Nature provides," she answered

matter-of-factly.

"I see." He glanced at the area around him. "Just what part of this nature are we going to eat?"

"Follow me." Dani gestured for him to follow her off the beaten path. She began to search the ground nearby and found a morel mushroom. "These are morels."

Isaak stooped down to pick a few and was just about to pop one in his mouth when Dani stopped him. She didn't mean for him to pop them in his mouth. "Don't eat that raw. Not unless you want to spend the rest of your trip in the bushes."

"So, no raw mushrooms." Isaak glanced at the bushes.

"Put these in your bag, and we'll cook them later." Dani reached down, picked a few mushrooms up, and handed them to Isaak. Then she leaned over and pulled some berries from a wild blueberry bush.

"These you can eat right now." Dani held a blueberry up and popped it into her mouth.

Isaak ate a blueberry too. "These are good."

"I'll show you a few other things too." The land was giving in many ways. Dani had learned how to live off of it long ago. Her father wanted to ensure she knew her roots and respected the earth for all its bounty.

Isaak snapped a few pictures of the blueberry bush. He turned to the mushrooms that were still left on the ground and took a few photos of those too. Dani could feel the camera turn on her right before he looked up at the trees above them.

"Don't you have anything better to do?" Isaak glared up at the trees.

"What's that?" Dani wondered what he was going on about now.

Isaak gestured to the bird in the trees. "We have a stalker."

"Well, hello there," Dani called up to the bird.

"Do you think it's the same bird?"

"Maybe. Hard to say." Dani believed that it was possible because ravens were such sacred creatures. They were a symbol of creation and transformation. Dani often felt like they were watching the world around them with a sense of curiosity and a hint of mischief, especially for those who didn't have the same respect for them.

Isaak grabbed a few blueberries and tried to catch a few. He missed, and the blueberries bounced off the ground. Isaak glanced up at the bird overhead. "Why does it look like he's laughing at me?"

Dani raised her hands and shrugged. "I mean...."

"It must be hard for you."

His words confused her at first. "What?"

"Dealing with people like me. People who have no clue what they're doing."

Dani smiled. It was true. Dealing with people who had no clue what they were doing outside the city limits was often annoying. Sometimes they surprised her, though, like Isaak. He was prepared to follow this through, even if it made him look like an idiot. Not that she thought of him that way. It was quite the opposite. Dani appreciated the way he soaked everything in. "It has its moments. But it's not so bad."

Dani smiled at him and stepped closer. "Hold still...."

Isaak froze immediately. "Why? Is there another snake?"

Dani watched him swallow uncomfortably as she stood less than a foot away from him. She lifted her hand and wiped away some of the blueberry juice that had dripped down his chin. When she did, her eyes locked with his, and she was drawn in despite her need to keep her distance. Dani felt the overwhelming need to see just what his lips might taste like with a hint of blueberry. She was desperately trying to shove those thoughts far away from her.

A loud caw interrupted them. The raven overhead punctuated the moment with his loud crowing again, breaking the moment. Dani stepped away from him, mentally slapping herself for getting too close to him in the first place. That was a disaster waiting to happen. If she let herself get close to him, she would be the one hurting in the end. He would go back to the city, and she'd never see him again.

"We should keep foraging." Dani put several feet between them.

Isaak started to look for more signs of vegetation. He stopped to glare at the bird. "I'm starting to think you really don't like me."

Dani stopped herself from laughing out loud. The bird continued to ignore him while he started grooming its feathers. Dani was finding this almost as entertaining as watching the locals try to play darts when they were three sheets to the wind. "Just a few more hours, and we'll make camp for the night."

"Just a few, huh?" Isaak shook his head and let out a long sigh.

"Don't worry. You'll make it," promised Dani.

"Or you'll have to carry me," countered Isaak.

"You'll make it." Dani waved off his words. She'd cut him off at the pass with that idea. "I'll give you a few more minutes to take a break and eat a few more berries, but then we're back on the trail."

The next leg of the trail went fast. Dani was surprised at how well Isaak had kept up with her. She could see him wince every once in a while when his foot dug into the ground too much. Tonight she would have to pull out the first aid kit and help him deal with the blisters that were already festering on his feet. This was why it was always a good idea to break in new boots slowly before taking on such a monstrous excursion. He wouldn't have known that, though, having never been on a hike like this before.

Now, the sky was orange from the sun that was setting in the sky. They had stopped for the night. Dani was making a small, cleared circle on the ground to make a fire. The goal was to leave as little imprint on the world when they were gone, so they would need to clear a small circle and ensure the fire was burned out well enough to not cause any future problems for the animals or their environment.

Isaak brought an armload of sticks and plopped them on the ground next to her. "Is that enough?"

"Hardly. We need thicker branches, Isaak. These will burn down way too fast. These are still too green. Look here...." Dani peeled the bark from the stick in her hand, showing him the fresh green coloring underneath. She pulled at the twig to bend it halfway as he watched her. "You want a stick you can snap easily. That means it's been drying out longer. See how it's hard to break it in half?"

Isaak reached down to get another stick and broke it in his hand. "Like this one?"

"Exactly. Find a lot more of those."

"I'm on it," promised Isaak. He turned around to do her bidding.

The sky was dark when they got a good fire going. The stars were just trying to poke through the stray clouds. The air around them was filled with the sounds of crickets and a few birds that were tucking in for the night. Dani was tending to a small pan over the fire. In it, she was cooking the morels, leeks, and the kelp that she had gathered earlier, using a metal spoon to move the food around so that it cooked evenly.

"So that's what you were keeping that for." Isaak was impressed with her skills.

"Kelp is a great source of fiber, vitamins, and minerals." It wasn't the best tasting thing in the world, but it sure beat digging for bugs.

"It smells delicious," complimented Isaak. He was sitting by the fire with a notebook in his hand. He was taking a few notes and appeared to be creating a few sketches.

Dani saw the calm that seemed to settle over him. She was glad he could let go of some of the stress he had started the journey with. When he first stepped into the bar, he was like a tightly wound coil ready to either spring into the air or crumble into tiny pieces. Gone were the stiff jawline and the dark eyes. In their place was a relaxed smile and eyes that seemed far less hollow. Dani wondered if he realized how restorative nature was.

"We'll eat some of the tack with it for our protein. Here, finish cooking this, and I'll get the rest of our meal out." Dani held the spoon up for Isaak.

She watched him set his book and pen on the ground. When Isaak took the spoon, his fingers brushed her own, and Dani felt a slight tingle where they touched. Her eyes met his, and she saw he was affected as well. She cleared her throat and retracted her hand before anything else could happen. Turning to her bag, she tried to keep her emotions in check. Just because she felt a spark didn't mean a damned thing.

Dani retrieved some hardtack pouches out of her backpack. They were not the most edible thing in the world, but they worked in a pinch. She actually preferred the fresh bounty from the land, but this was what they had at the moment, and it would have to do. She ripped one of the packs open and sprinkled the contents into the pan.

Isaak continued to stir the contents in the pan. His nose crinkled when he saw the hardtack. "I hope that tastes better than it looks."

"Don't worry, it will." Dani's thoughts wandered

as Isaak continued to cook over the fire. She couldn't hold on to even one thought. She was distracted by his proximity. When she turned back to look at him, she could tell the food was ready. "Let's take it off the fire now."

"You got it." Isaak pulled the pan off the fire and set it on the ground between them.

Dani scooped some of it out of the pan into the empty pouch and handed it to Isaak. Then she handed him a fork. "Try some."

Isaak blew on the food before he brought a forkful to his mouth. His eyebrows rose in surprise. "This is good. See? Who needs a five-star restaurant? My compliments to the chef. Who taught you all of this?"

"My father. He learned it from his father and so on. It's something that's been passed down since the beginning of time."

Isaak was thoughtful before he spoke. "Is this it for you?"

"What do you mean?" Dani wondered where he was going with this line of questions.

"What do you see yourself doing ten years from

now?"

Dani tilted her head and looked into the fire. "I haven't given it much thought, I suppose. Take over the businesses for my father, perhaps."

"And what does he do?" asked Isaak.

Dani grinned. "You've met him. He owns the Blue Moon Bar."

Understanding dawned on Isaak quickly. "So, I have. And does he give tours too?"

"Sometimes, but he spends most of his time at the bar." Her father was more wrapped up in the bar than outside these days. Sometimes she wondered if investing in a business was the best course for her father. In her opinion, he was meant to be in the great outdoors, just like her. Having cancer and running a bar wasn't a good combination either. That's why she helped him as much as she could. Family was the most important thing in her life. More important than any of her other relationships by far.

"So, no other expectations out of life? What about your other half?" prodded Isaak.

"What other half?" Dani tried to push the question away. Part of her was flattered that he asked it. The other half was terrified that it meant he was interested because there was a small part of her that returned that interest. She couldn't afford that indulgence.

"Living the single life, then?" Isaak was surprised.

"Until I have a reason not to? What about you?" Turnabout was fair play, right?

"Been a free agent for most of my life. I'm too driven for relationships. Nothing serious at the moment," answered Isaak.

"So, you're a writer. How's that working for you?" Dani turned the tables on him. Maybe it was time to put him under the microscope and see how he liked it.

Isaak grinned. "It has its moments."

"Like what?"

"Being schooled by a beautiful woman," teased Isaak.

Dani shook her head. "Flattery will get you nowhere."

Isaak shrugged. "A guy has to try."

Now, that sounded like all the other men she had run into before. They always had to try something. If he kept that up, she really would leave him out here in the forest. Let the raven lead him home. "Eat up. Best get some rest too. We have a long day tomorrow."

Chapter 9

The forest was thick in the area where they had camped, and a little mist covered the floor as the early morning air was filled with wet wonder. The sun would be heating it up soon enough, for it was going to be another beautiful day. Isaak was taking in the world around him. The more time he spent in the Great Bear Rainforest, the less he felt like an outsider. He'd actually slept well last night. At least this morning, Dani didn't give him grief about snoring. Either he hadn't, or she was being kind in not mentioning it. The dark circles under her eyes implied the latter.

Isaak watched her as she forged ahead of him, making her own trail. She was so serious most of the time. Isaak was fairly serious, but Dani was surrounded by this cloud that he couldn't seem to wade through, just like this morning fog. He could see just enough ahead of him not to fall into some nature trap. He saw Dani stop and quickly did the same, so he didn't run into her again.

Dani pointed out a blacktail deer in the distance. "Look."

Isaak turned to where she pointed and lifted his camera. He snapped a few pictures until the deer realized their presence and hopped away. He had a few questions he wanted to ask, but at this point, he was more convinced that the best course would be to save his energy. Plus, Dani was not in a very talkative mood. He'd not get much conversation out of her. So he continued to trek after, taking in all the sights of the Great Bear Rainforest as he did. The forest, the Bella Coola River, which could be seen from the edge of a cliff, and the mountains in the distance were sights he would never forget.

By late afternoon, Dani had decided to stop for a while. At first, Isaak was a little worried. Especially when she told him that they were going to fish. Isaak had only fished a handful of times, and each time, he had used a fishing pole. There was definitely no fishing pole in his backpack. Isaak was pretty sure he would have seen it before now if there had been. The fact that there were now standing a few feet from a medium-sized stream that ran through a clearing in the forest was a driving force on whatever happened next. The stream's bed had rocks in the middle, and there were a few good-sized rocks along the shore. It was almost as if the man upstairs had just plopped it down in the middle of nowhere.

Isaak watched Dani whittle a few sticks. She was making the sticks into small spears that they could catch fish with, and while it was impressive, Isaak was pretty sure no matter how sharp the point was, he was not going to be able to catch one. Even so, he was not about to turn down a challenge. Even the folly of this adventure would be entertaining to his readers. Maybe that should be his niche, heading out into survival situations and testing his mettle no matter how confident he was in his abilities. His success or failures would definitely keep the subscribers reading along.

Dani set one of the sticks down on the ground. She held the other one in her hand with the sharpened point turned down to the ground. "I'll step out across the rocks to the middle of the creek. Fish settle around the rocks."

"What do you want me to do?" Isaak asked her.

"Just watch what I do. When you think you can handle it, you'll give it a try."

Isaak could watch her. Hell, if he was given a chance, he'd make that a hobby. She was very easy on the eyes. There was something about this woman. No matter how aloof she tried to be, she seemed to call that more attention to herself. He watched her balance on a rock in the middle of the creek. Her spear was raised up to her hip as she peered into the depths of the icy water. Her spear sliced through the water and impaled a fish in one swift move.

"You got it! That looks easy enough," Isaak called to her.

Dani turned to shore and carefully stepped from rock to rock until she was back on the shore. She smiled at him with just a tint of mischief. "Easy? Care to place a wager on that?"

Isaak pretended to be confident. "What do you have in mind?"

"Whoever gets the most fish can relax through dinner. The loser has to clean the fish, cook dinner and clean up afterwards." Dani pulled a fish stringer out of her backpack and put the fish on the stringer.

"You already have a head start," grumbled Isaak.

Dani grinned at him. "This one won't count."

Isaak put his hand out to shake on it. "Deal!"

Dani laughed and shook his hand before heading back to the water. She turned around and sat down on one of the rocks while she waited for him to head out to the water. Pulling out her knife, she whittled another branch while she sat there. "I'll just wait here and give you a little head start."

"A head start?"

"Yeah. You're going to need it," teased Dani.

Isaak laughed at her challenge. "Oh, it's on!" He climbed on the rocks and hopped from rock to rock until he found a good perching spot. His shoes took on a little water, but they were quality boots, so they wouldn't fall apart on him from just a little water. He was more concerned about slipping on the rocks. As if to punctuate his point, his footing wobbled slightly.

"Careful there, hot shot!" Dani called out to him.

Isaak gave her an irritated glance. "Thanks…."

Dani chuckled. "Not as easy as it looks, is it?"

He waived her off. "You keep sharpening that stick and leave the fishing to me. I'm going to win this bet," he taunted her.

Still amused, Dani returned to sharpening the branch. "Uh-huh. The way you're going, all you're going to catch is a cold."

Isaak shot her another irritated glance. Was she going to pick on him the whole time? He could tell she was really enjoying this. Her grin grew into a full-blown smile, and her eyes twinkled as she motioned for him to carry on with a wave of her hand.

Figures. She had to catch the fish first thing and then watch him most likely fail. Well, he'd show her. Isaak returned to his task. Raising the spear, he plunged it into the water, totally missing the fish. The force he used was so strong and determined that he slipped and fell backward into the stream with a loud splash.

Alarmed, Dani jumped to her feet. "Isaak!"

Isaak surfaced from beneath the water, blowing water as he broke through the surface. The water was only waist-deep. He stood up, shaking water from himself. His expression was pure disgust. Well, he certainly showed her, didn't he?

When Dani realized he was not hurt, she started laughing. "You missed!"

Isaak shook his head in irritation, gave it a second thought and then started laughing with her. He had learned early in life that it was better to laugh through the pain of any embarrassment. While this stung a little more, mostly because he was soaking wet, Isaak knew he would recover. This was only a bump in the road and would certainly make for an entertaining segway in the story.

He was anything if determined, so Isaak got back up and tried again. And again, and yet again. Isaak had lost count of how many times he had shoved his spear into the water. At least he stayed upright those times. Dani had just speared another fish. It was second nature to her.

She held the flopping fish up triumphantly. "That makes two for me. Where's yours?"

Isaak held up a finger. "One. That makes one for you. You said the other didn't count."

"Still one up on you, city slicker," teased Dani.

Isaak shook his head. "Don't get cocky, sweetheart."

Dani was taken aback by his words. "Sweetheart?"

Isaak was watching the water carefully for a fish. "If you can call me city slicker, I can call you sweetheart."

Isaak let the spear fly into the water. He overshot his target, and the movement caused his foot to slip on the rock. Isaak went into the water, which was probably even more aggravating because he had almost dried off from the first time. He came back up, sputtering. Would he ever catch a break? "Sonofa."

Dani started to laugh so hard that she lost her footing on the rocks too. A loud splash followed her as she fell back into the water. "Ah!"

He waded over to Dani and helped her up. The two of them were now laughing together with the ease of a couple who had been together long enough not to take themselves seriously. Isaak was lost in the moment when he brushed Dani's wet hair away from her eyes. He kissed her playfully on the cheek. "That just made my day."

Dani pushed him away playfully. "Not one of my finer moments."

Isaak grinned at her. "It was perfect."

Dani handed him the spear floating next to her. "Keep fishing, Mr. Lee."

"I thought I was." He took the spear and turned up his charm. Isaak went back to the rock and held the spear in his hand again.

Dani turned away from him, ignoring his words as she found a place to sit down. She was combing out her wet hair while she watched his attempts to catch any of the fish that swam in the stream under him. "I sure hope you're a good cook."

Isaak didn't even bother to turn around. He spied a fish and was prepared to attack. "Stop gloating. You haven't won yet. Besides, I believe I'll have this one any second."

Dani opened her mouth to come up with a witty retort when she spied a large black bear lumbering in Isaak's direction from the woods. She slowly stood up and held a hand up to get his attention, but Isaak was focused on his attack. "Isaak."

Isaak barely looked up at her. "Stop distracting me. It won't work."

Dani's voice was filled with forced calm. "Uh, Isaak?"

"Just. Another. Second…." What was she trying to do, throw the game here? Not going to happen. Isaak threw the spear and finally captured the fish on the other end.

"I got it! Yeah!" Isaak hauled the spear out of the water and turned to face Dani. It had a large flopping fish on the end.

Dani was motioning behind him. Her face was slightly pale. His name came out in a whisper. "Isaak."

"Take that, sweetheart! We're tied, and it's bigger than yours!" hooted Isaak. He turned to see Dani waving her arms with a panic-stricken look on her face. "What?"

"What?"

A loud roar erupted behind him, and Isaak spun around to see the black bear on the other shore that was now standing on his hind legs. He had never been this close to anything so large and menacing before in his life. It was a miracle that he hadn't fallen back into the water again. "Oh, God!"

"Remain calm. He wants your fish," Dani calmly reminded him.

"So do I," complained Isaak.

"If that's another attempt at humor, it's not funny, Isaak."

The bear roared its challenge again. Dani gestured at the fish on the spear. "Slowly lower the fish to the rock and make your way to the shore. Don't make eye contact, and don't turn your back on the bear."

Isaak lowered the fish to the rock, even though he wanted to keep his catch of the day. The damn bear could have let him take a picture of his catch first before he bullied him out of it. Ah, well, perhaps there would be another chance. While Isaak carefully backed away from the bear, Dani gathered their things. By the time Isaak made it to shore, the bear was at the rock, eating Isaak's fish.

"Let's go," whispered Dani. She handed Isaak his backpack and shoes before they both headed back into the forest.

They had decided to put plenty of space between

them and the hungry bear. Isaak followed Dani deeper into the rainforest, too distracted by the earlier escapades. How could he not be? His heart was still racing hours later, but that could have been from all the walking they were doing too.

His feet were definitely feeling the burn today. Isaak realized now why they always said to break in shoes slowly before using them long-term. While these boots were the right size and fit perfectly, they still didn't have the give that was required when logging this many miles each day. He wondered if Dani had anything for the blisters that made his heels feel like they were on fire.

By the time they were ready to settle down for the night, Isaak was beyond exhausted. How was Dani unaffected by all the walking? She looked like she had just taken a stroll around the block. He wasn't a lightweight where exercise was concerned, but she sure made him feel like a novice in many things. At least he had been able to make the fire himself tonight. Isaak had always been a quick study. The cleaned fish were sitting on the rock next to them.

"Are you sure it's safe to cook this here?" he

asked her.

"For the ninth time, it's safe, Isaak," she placated him.

"No bears?"

"I can't guarantee that. Great Bear Rainforest is filled with them. Hence the name," she reminded him.

"I know that. I did do some research before I came. Are there more bears here because of the sanctions?" Isaak had only been able to learn so much when it came to the bears inside the forest here, considering the lack of time to prepare for the trip.

"There tends to be. One of the reasons hunting isn't allowed is because of the Spirit Bear." Dani was scanning the trees around them.

"A white bear born to a black Kermode bear?" Isaak had read about them more than once in his lifetime. Their occurrence was a quandary. There was no rhyme or reason as to when or why one was born.

"You know your facts. But they're so much more than bears. They're a symbol to many of us." Dani looked like she was prepared to give him a full-on lecture.

"They're very rare, so rare, hardly anyone has a

record of them. Have you ever seen one?"

Dani gave him a nervous glance. "Some things are best left unsaid."

"You have seen one." He took her answer for what it meant. She had seen one before, but for some reason, she didn't feel safe disclosing that information. Dani was protective. Perhaps she felt she had a reason to be.

"Just cook the fish." Dani got up from the fire and walked out into the trees, leaving Isaak alone.

"So. That's clearly a touchy subject." That's just great. Now he'd gone and done it. He'd have to cook the fish all by himself and pray he didn't burn it. Over the stovetop or a grill, he had more control over the cooking process, but a campfire didn't have a way to control the amount of blaze. He'd have to time it perfectly, or they would be eating charred fish tonight.

Dani came back just about the time the fish was ready. The lucky girl didn't have to involve herself with any of the cooking. Even though she technically won the bet, Isaak felt a little jilted. It wasn't his fault the bear had decided to chase them off. He'd have to ask for a rematch soon. He watched her sit down a few feet away from him. Isaak realized he had hit a nerve earlier. "I'm sorry for earlier."

Dani sighed, and her face softened. "It's not your fault you don't understand. I've spent half my life under these trees. I know them so well, I almost can hear their voices."

"And what do they say to you?" He was truly curious as to what her answer would be.

"To protect the things that others would destroy. To give back to our Earth instead of always taking away. To protect our treasures, like these bears."

"It's hard to keep that mentality when you are surrounded by concrete. It's easier to see why it's important when you're out here." Isaak handed her a piece of fish.

"I guess that's why I'll never trade in my freedom here for that kind of prison." She took a bite of the fish and swallowed it.

"I'm sorry you feel that way. City life isn't so bad. There are plenty of places to eat, and everything I want is virtually at my fingertips." Isaak felt like he had to defend his life choices. Why did he suddenly feel so materialistic?

"What you want and need are sometimes two separate things."

"We'll probably never agree on that." That was a sad thought to him. Isaak thought they were forming a connection. Not that he had expected to do so, it had simply happened.

"That is something we can agree on." Dani turned away from him and looked up at the skies. "You and I are very different. Let's just drop it. It's a beautiful night."

Isaak was not looking at the stars. Instead, he was appreciating the way the moon framed her face as she looked up. "Yes, beautiful."

Dani turned to glance at him and caught him staring at her. Their eyes met for a moment before she broke the connection. The moment was lost as she pulled away. "I'm going to call it a night."

"Night." Isaak watched her slide into her sleeping bag and turn away. He gazed up at the stars to see what she was looking at. The stars above were scattered through the canopy of trees, but their bright dots could still be seen.

In the tree above them, the raven was looking

down on them. Neither one of them saw the bird as it tucked into its wings and nuzzled its beak.

Chapter 10

Night had already come and gone. Thankfully, Dani had woken up more refreshed. There came the point in time where the body just decided it was time to sleep, no matter how many distractions were trying to get in its way. Isaak was definitely a distraction. If she had known he would pull her in so easily, she would have tried to find someone else to take him on the trip. Of course, very few who knew this trek the way she did were willing to take an amateur along with them. Could she request older, less attractive men next time? Maybe a group of women?

The thing about Isaak was he wasn't always trying to woo her with his charm. It was the ease with which he took in the world around him that she found so damn attractive. He might look like Jason, but Jason had never really cared for the great outdoors. That man had been driven to find a life anywhere but here. Jason had thought she would go with him. He had been mistaken. Dani couldn't leave her father. She was the only person he had left.

Dani glanced over at Isaak, who was now using a stick he found along the way, a makeshift walking stick. His camera hung absently around his neck as he took in the world around him through his eyes, not a lens. They were walking side by side, and Dani couldn't figure out if she had slowed her pace or if he had finally figured out how to walk a little faster.

"Caw!"

The loud crowing above them caught her attention. Dani paused, then stopped abruptly. Something felt off. She looked up at the bird, then down under the tree it was perched on. "Hold on."

"What is it?" Isaak stood in his spot, waiting for an answer that Dani couldn't quite give yet.

Dani walked to a spot near one of the trees. She dropped to a knee and started to explore the ground nearby, and when she saw the imprint on the ground, she smiled and looked up at the raven. "Thanks, friend."

"Dani?"

Dani turned to look up at him. "A bear track."

Isaak seemed nonplussed by her discovery as if his one encounter with a bear had made him a professional in dealing with them. "Probably one of many."

"Let me guess, it stole your food?" Isaak glanced up to the raven and started to chide it. The bird shifted its feet but didn't reply.

"It's injured." Dani saw the drops of blood near the tracks.

Isaak gave her a quizzical look. "The bird? He looks fine to me."

"No, the bear." Dani tried to hang onto her nerves. Was the bear still alive? Were the hunters still around? Gone was the peace from earlier. She had been enjoying the forest with its gentle energy. In its place was a heavy fog of trepidation. Dani felt the hairs rise on the back of her neck at the situation.

"How do you know that?" Isaak was trying

to see what she saw, but he just couldn't follow her thought process.

Dani pointed to the small track of blood on the ground. "See?"

"Then we should head in the opposite direction, right?"

Dani frowned. That would be the easy way out. Dani had never taken the easy way. "We need to find it."

Isaak looked at her like she had lost her mind. "Are you crazy? Why?"

"Crazy? For wanting to find out what happened to it? Don't be an ass, Isaak." Why did men only think of themselves? Couldn't he see there was a much bigger picture here? He was looking a little less attractive.

"Why? Because I was always told not to poke a bear? You have heard of the expression, right?"

"Yes, but in this instance, I would disregard it." Dani admitted to herself that he did have a point. It was a dangerous situation. It wasn't like they were tracking down a squirrel.

"What's different about this? It's injured, probably in pain, and ready to attack anything that gets in its way. I don't need a lifetime of experience in the woods to know an injured animal can turn on everything in its path." Isaak was almost gesturing with his walking stick at this point.

"Because this bear wasn't injured in a natural way. It was shot." Her words made her feel a little helpless. She wished she could have prevented it from happening in the first place. Unfortunately, there was only so much she could do to stop these poachers. All she could do was try to take care of the aftermath.

"How could you possibly know that?" Isaak was surprised. He peered down at the tracks, confusion still on his face. "Are the tracks speaking to you?"

"If you're done mocking me...." Dani pointed to a piece of coppery metal to the right of them.

Isaak was visibly impressed. "I wasn't mocking you. I'm just trying to understand. How did you see that?"

"Time, training. I spent half my life out here, Isaak. I know what to look for. This isn't the first time I've come across an injured bear. We've spent years trying to protect the bears here. Somehow, they always find a way to destroy them."

"Poachers?" asked Isaak.

"Yes, and overconfident ones at that." Dani was so mad she could spit. When will these people stop destroying innocent creatures? Dani walked over to the bullet casing and picked it up. Then she turned with a determined look on her face. "Well, Isaak, you wanted to learn about outdoor survival. You're about to get the extreme edition."

"Why do I get the feeling I'm not going to like this?"

Dani gave him a half-smile. "Don't worry. I'll make it up to you."

His eyebrows rose curiously. "How's that?"

"I'll show you one of my favorite places." Dani flashed him a smile that made Isaak's resolve soften.

"Fine, but if he tries to eat me, I'm not going to let you hear the end of it. So, what's the plan?"

"We'll track it down and call it in." Dani patted the satellite phone attached to Isaak's pack.

"Couldn't we just call it in here?" Isaak didn't look like he was ready to set one foot after the bear.

"It's not enough for them to come to the scene of the crime. We have to find him." Dani wished it were that easy, but it was best to know where the bear was before attempting to call it in. That would make the rescue that much faster if the bear was able to be saved. Most times, it was just a body retrieval or a dead end completely. It was rare for hunters to leave their prey in the woods. Although some of them enjoyed the thrill of the chase and took their time felling their target.

"Fine. Let's do it." Isaak didn't look like he was even remotely ready to do anything other than run in the other direction, but at least he was trying.

"Are you agreeing because you want to impress me or because you're afraid I'll leave you stranded in the middle of nowhere?" Dani asked him.

Isaak grinned at her. "No comment...."

"Caw!" Apparently, the raven had to throw in his two cents again.

Isaak glared up at him. "I've had just about enough of you."

Dani shook her head at Isaak. "You know he doesn't understand you, right?"

"Says you. I've got the feeling we understand each other well enough." Isaak pointed to his eyes, then back at the bird. "I've got my eyes on you."

Dani nodded for Isaak to follow her and was glad when he did so with no more complaints. Dani continued to follow the trail the bear had left. Its tracks seemed to wind through the trees, almost as if the bear were driven by his pain. She could understand that feeling of fear and paranoia that must have clouded his brain. Blood punctuated every few tracks, which told her that the wound was still bleeding. While the blood was in smaller droplets, it was still imperative that they find the bear sooner than later.

As she continued to track it, she found a few other tracks that were not made by any wild animal. They were footprints, boot-sized, maybe size nines or larger. Dani paused and pointed to the set of tracks. "It's being followed by at least two people."

Isaak bent down and inspected the footprints. He ran his hand across it. "By the size of them, I'd say they are pretty tall."

Dani was impressed with his intuition. "How do you know that?"

"I watch a lot of true crime shows. They always say something like that."

Dani's head fell back in feigned annoyance. She

shook her head at him and sighed. "Alright, Columbo, let's keep moving."

Isaak shrugged and held his hands up. "What?"

"Come on." Dani nodded for him to follow her. At least he had his hiking legs under him now. His heels had blistered just as she predicted, but he had learned to toughen up and push through it. Dani admired that. Not everyone could do that. It took a lot of determination.

"Do you think we will find it alive?" asked Isaak.

"I don't know." She wished she had the answer to that, but the fact of the matter was that the signs weren't pointing to a good outcome right now. Nevertheless, she wouldn't let some damned poachers confiscate another bear from the Great Bear Rainforest. It was more than principle at this point. Dani was driven to protect the animals and their environment. If she ever did leave her father's side, that is the kind of work she would like to do. She actually had connections with the World Animal Protection organization. For now, she did what she could in her small corner of the world. Every little thing helped.

"What if we don't find it?" Gone was Isaak's

playful smile. His concern was surprising.

"Then all you have lost is a few hours traipsing in the forest with me." She didn't want to have the real talk with him and explain what would have happened to the bear if they didn't find it. It was heartbreaking to think about.

Isaak shrugged. "We were already here."

Dani let out a small sigh of relief. She had been worried about how he would react to the detour. His reaction was everything she needed it to be. Definitely a redeeming quality, one of many she was discovering despite her need to keep him in an untouchable box. She was really starting to like the man. "Thank you, Isaak."

His eyebrows arched in surprise. "For what?"

"Humoring me."

Isaak gave her a charming smile. "Like you said, I don't have much choice. I'd be lost without you."

"I would have come back for you," She assured him.

"Would you?" He looked a little dubious.

"Of course."

"Just doing your job." He was teasing her a little,

but there was almost a question in there too.

Dani felt an awkward moment pass between them as they both had thoughts that they weren't quite prepared to voice. How could she admit to having feelings when he was just going to leave anyway? Besides, she hardly knew the man. This wasn't some fairytale happy ever after love story. This was a job, plain and simple. Speaking of which, daylight was going to be wasting here soon. They would have to keep moving if they were going to catch sight of the bear. She broke the eye contact and put a few steps between them. "Precisely."

Dani reached down to touch the leaf next to her. "Blood's still fresh. We can't be far now."

Isaak didn't say another word. He just fell into step beside her, following the trail that only she could see. Dani pushed forward, not only determined to find the bear but desperate to put space between them before she did something she would regret.

Chapter 11

The night was settling over the forest. Very few animals were rustling in the darkness. Instead, a loud bunch of voices erupted, breaking the stillness. Four men were sitting around a blazing fire celebrating their daily spoils. They had been hunting in the Great Bear Rainforest all afternoon and had finally managed to hit a bear. Not only had they lined the target in their sights, but they had also been able to do so without any of those pesky rangers catching on to them. Now, they just had to track down the beast and finish it off.

The first hunter, John, was in his mid-forties. He tipped the beer and held it back until he had swallowed the last drop. Then he tossed the empty can on the ground and gestured to Jake to give him another. "Toss me a cold one, will ya?"

In his early twenties, Jake was the youngest in the group. This was his first hunting trip with the others. "Catch," said Jake as he tossed the beer at John, who barely caught it. He reached into the cooler to retrieve another beer for himself and sat down in a folding chair.

John glared at Jake when he popped the top, and foam spewed from the can and dripped down his fingers. "Not so hard next time," grumbled John.

Jake shrugged as he popped the top on his own beer. "Sorry, Bro, my bad." Jake took a sip of his own beer and held it up in salute.

Ryan sat back in his chair and glared at both men. He was in his fifties and was a grisly-looking man with a beard that covered his face and hung well past his chin. "Maybe you should both slow down a bit."

Chris let out a loud belch which had John and Jake chuckling. He held his beer up to the two men and smirked at Ryan. "You're just afraid we'll get to it before you do."

Ryan pointed a beefy finger at Chris, then

motioned his finger to include the other two. "Don't get cocky on me. What we're doing is risky," chided Ryan. "If the rangers catch us, we'll all be locked up."

John let out a derisive snort. "You worry too much. Just think about all the money we'll get from the spoils. The gallbladder alone will bring us a small fortune on the black market," John reminded him. "Drink up. Ain't gonna get far with that wound."

"Even so, we best remain on guard. A wounded bear is no laughing matter," Ryan growled. Ryan bared his chest to show a nasty scar from a prior encounter with a wounded grizzly. "It might serve you better to keep your wits about you."

"Yes, Daddy," Chris mocked, and the other two laughed.

"I ain't your damned daddy." That comment had the others laughing hard. Ryan shook his head and joined in the drunken laughter.

~*~

A little further away, Dani and Isaak were looking for a place to make camp. Well, Dani was. Isaak was doing his best to pretend he knew exactly what kind of spot she was looking for. He knew she was the professional here, and considering there was a wounded bear somewhere nearby, he was relatively sure she would pick a spot that would be at a safe distance from it.

The wind rustled through the trees, and Isaak looked up to ensure the raven wasn't following him again. He still couldn't figure out if that thing was being helpful or just giving him a hard time. His money was on the latter because that bird had tried to hit him several times with his projective poop. Dodging defecating birds wasn't something he signed up for. Hell, he hadn't signed for any of these things, especially the alluring woman standing next to him. She was the kind of woman that made him want to rethink his ways. The type of woman he could see himself settling down with someday. His mother would approve, especially since she was so good at dressing him down. She'd always said he needed a queen to rule his roost.

As they searched for a decent spot, the sounds of muffled laughter drifted in on the breeze. Dani raised her hand and whispered, "Did you hear that?"

He paused to listen. "What was that?" Isaak took her que and spoke quietly in return.

"It could be the hunters." Dani started to head in

that direction, but Isaak pulled on her arm.

"Just what are you doing?" Isaak had a feeling this was going to be a night he wouldn't forget. If she was going to do what he thought she was, they would be lucky if they survived it.

Dani turned to face Isaak, her expression grave and determined. "Going to get a closer look."

That's what he was afraid of. Was she out of her mind? Other than the hunting knife she carried, Dani was unarmed as far as he knew. That wouldn't help much against firearms. "Is that a good idea?" He wasn't sure why he wasted his breath.

"Do you have a better idea?" Dani crossed her arms over her chest as she waited to see what he would come up with.

Isaak wasn't about to take her bait right now. He might not know much about survival in the woods, but his street instincts told him to let it be. They were clearly outnumbered. This was a serious situation, one that made him want to run in the other direction. "Yeah, stay away and stay alive. They could be dangerous."

Dani brushed his words away. "It could be nothing. You worry too much. It could be other hikers and might not even be them."

"And if it is?" Isaak couldn't help thinking that this was a very bad idea.

Dani shrugged. "We'll figure it out."

"Why am I not convinced?" He looked up to the trees and spied the raven. Isaak shook his head at the bird. "I know you put her up to this."

Dani turned around to chastise him. "Stop talking to the bird, and come on."

Isaak pointed in the direction of the laughter. "Just for the record, I think this is a bad idea."

Dani shot him an exasperated glance. "Noted, now, let's go."

Isaak followed Dani deeper into the darkness. Carefully placing each footstep to avoid detection. Isaak could hear his heart pumping loud in his ears and was pretty sure every living thing around them could hear the same thing. He enjoyed a good crime show any day of the week, just never expected to be part of one.

As they approached the poacher camp, Dani gestured for him to stay where he was while she went to check out the other side. He wasn't too thrilled about the idea, but she was in charge, and by how she was acting, she had done this a time or two.

In the camp below, Isaak saw three poachers outlined by the glow of a campfire. They were drinking and joking around like they didn't have a care in the world. Honestly, Isaak found his blood boiling just a bit. From what Dani had told him throughout this trip, hunters like these were a major problem in the area, even though there were laws in place to prevent them from hunting here. Why did people always feel they were exempt from the law?

From behind the trees, Isaak took his camera out and started taking photos of the men gathered around the campfire. The camera made a soft click that Dani heard from her hiding spot. She held up a finger to caution him. Isaak was surprised at how well she blended in with the trees. He could barely see her and was fairly certain that none of the hunters would be able to either.

They could faintly hear the men's voices over the short distance from their hiding spots. The men were loud, drunk, and possibly armed and dangerous, a deadly combination. Isaak crept just a little closer to hear their conversation.

"Ever see a bear run so far?" asked John.

Chris gestured to Jake. "Yeah, almost as fast as our boy Jake when that bull chased him out of the pen," teased Chris.

Jake appeared indignant. "Says you. I was leading him right where I wanted him," added Jake.

"Ha! All you needed was a bulls-eye tattooed on that ass of yours. He'd a had ya," said Chris.

"In your dreams. You need another beer?" asked Jake.

"It won't make me forget how you near froze your toe off last winter. Ice fishing…not your thing," remembered Chris.

"You're a bunch of drunken idiots. Where'd Ryan head off to?" asked John.

"Takin' a leak," answered Chris.

Isaak glanced over at Dani and saw her holding up four fingers before pointing down to the three below. Isaak shifted a little and moved to a closer tree to get a better shot of the men around the fire. He snapped several more pictures, making sure to capture the rifles that were leaning against the trees. Zooming in on the faces, he took closeups of each hunter. They may not bring these guys in, but they would at least be able to pass the photos along to the authorities.

As he crouched there, Isaak turned to look over at Dani and saw her gesturing behind him. Isaak was about to turn around to figure out what she was making a big deal about when he heard a loud click of what he could only assume was a rifle being cocked.

"Don't move, asshole," Ryan ordered, causing Isaak to freeze immediately in his spot. "Keep your hands where I can see 'em."

Isaak let the camera drop around his neck and slowly lifted his hands up. He glanced at Dani and slightly shook his head in warning, hoping she would understand. Isaak knew that she was well hidden. There was a good chance she would stay that way if she didn't try to intervene. Somehow he doubted she could stay out of it, but there was a small chance she would know better. There was no sense in both of them getting captured.

"Get up," ordered Ryan.

"I'm not armed," Isaak told him.

The hunter didn't seem to care. "Shut up. Turn

around."

"Relax," Isaak replied as he slowly complied with his commands.

"Turn toward the camp and walk." Isaak kept his hands up and started to walk.

Ryan stepped closer and roughly shoved Isaak on the shoulder, propelling him forward. Isaak stumbled but managed not to fall. Isaak chose not to look over at Dani. For now, she remained hidden in the trees. He would like to keep it that way. Isaak had no idea how he would get out of this situation, but more than anything, he wanted to keep her out of it. He couldn't imagine a world without her fierce spirit inside it. There would be a small hole if his life was snuffed out, but it would be immeasurable without her.

Immeasurable. Had any woman ever impacted him so greatly in such a short time? So much so that he was pondering the way she might fit permanently into his life while he was walking through a forest at gunpoint. He honestly couldn't think of any other woman he would have ever thought of in this situation. It was strange how his life goals seemed to be changing. Goal number one, get out of this alive.

Isaak tried not to trip as he walked down the small slope leading to their camp. Walking with his hands up was trickier than he thought it would be. Having his hands up made his balance off. Isaak felt like he was teetering down the hill but managed to keep himself upright by the skin of his teeth. When he got to the outskirts of their camp, Ryan shoved Isaak to his knees.

"Whatcha got there?" asked John.

"We got a problem." Ryan gestured to Isaak.

"Looks that way," added Chris.

"Wouldn't have been a problem if you boys had stayed sober. Pretty sure he heard everything," grumbled Ryan.

"What we gonna do with him?" asked Jake.

Ryan pointed his rifle down to the camera on Isaak's neck and nodded his head. "Hand it over."

Isaak hesitated. If he handed over the camera, all his work from the week would be gone. Not only that, the evidence he had captured would be gone too. He had to decide fast if his life was worth preserving all of that. Not to mention, how the hell was he supposed to win against four men. They might be drunk, but they were still armed and deadly.

"I'd listen to him if I was you. He can get downright nasty when you don't," warned Chris.

Isaak lifted the camera off his neck and held it up in front of him. At this moment, he might have blamed Dani for wanting to get closer to the camp. Most rational people might, but right now, he was angrier at these jerks who thought they were some kind of martial law. Then there was the concern that even handing over the camera wouldn't be enough. After all, he had seen their faces, and the more time he spent in their company, the easier it would be to pick them out of a lineup if he ever made it out of here alive.

"Toss it on the ground," ordered Ryan.

Isaak tossed the camera on the ground and looked back up at Ryan. "Anything else?"

Ryan nudged the barrel of the rifle into Isaak's shoulder. "Shut up, smartass and hand over the pack."

"You heard him. Nice and slow now," added John.

Isaak took the pack off his shoulders and slid it onto the ground. He was not keen on them taking ownership of his bag either. All his survival items were in there, and while he was still learning to use most of them, the thought of not having access to them made him nervous. Not to mention the satellite phone was attached to it. He was pretty sure if they wanted to find any kind of rescue support, the phone would be their only means to get it, especially since he hadn't been able to get any bars on his cell.

"Anyone else with him?" asked Chris.

"Not that I could see. Check his pockets," suggested Ryan.

Jake stepped over to Isaak and started to search his pockets. He pulled out his phone and wallet. He held up the phone with a drunken smile. "Someone's got money. I think I'll keep this one."

"Why, so they can track you?" Ryan shook his head in disgust.

"We can always take the SIM card out," suggested Chris.

"Won't matter much. Can't get any reception in most places here," added John.

Ryan poked Isaak with the barrel of his gun. "Who are you?"

"I'm a wildlife journalist. Just exploring the

rainforest," answered Isaak.

"By yourself?" John's head wobbled slightly as he tried to keep upright in his chair. He had definitely had way too much to drink.

"I'm good company." Isaak tried not to let his fear show. They already had the upper hand here. Letting them see his weakness wouldn't help. He had to stay strong to keep them away from Dani. Isaak prayed she had already gotten herself away from here.

"What should we do with him?" asked Chris.

"Kill him?" suggested John. There was a dark light in his eyes as if he had dreamed of doing just that since the moment Isaak stepped into the camp.

Isaak's eyes got wide, and his cheek clenched despite his resolve to not show any reaction. That man was completely homicidal. How many people had he killed? Was he a serial killer disguised as a drunken hunter? Isaak was no longer thinking about his article. That was for damned sure. Hell, he may never write again if these maniacs decided to pull the trigger.

"We can't do that, can we?" asked Jake.

"We have to keep all our options open. Besides, we can't just let 'em go. He knows too much," ordered

John.

"Tie him up for now. We'll figure it out in the morning," suggested Ryan.

Jake and Chris stepped over to where Isaak knelt. They each took an arm and pulled Isaak off the ground. Then they hauled him over to a tree. It wasn't that he was trying to defy them. His feet just didn't seem to want to work. Terror did that to a person. As they tied him to the tree, Isaak closed his eyes and tried to keep the thoughts from swirling inside him. Maybe there was still hope. If these drunken fools fell asleep, maybe he could find a way out of these ropes and get as far away from here as possible. The only problem with that was Isaak had no idea where the hell he was or how to find his way out of the Great Bear Rainforest to a place where he could find help. For now, he would take one breath at a time. Breathe, formulate a plan, and try to stay calm.

Chapter 12

From her perch, Dani could see everything going on inside the camp. Guilt crept up inside her. She was so focused on trying to save the bear she hadn't stopped to think of the risk she was putting Isaak in. He tried to stop her, but she was so pigheaded that she refused to listen. Now, these buffoons were contemplating more than just capturing Isaak. They might kill him. She had to do something, but what? Dani continued to watch to see if there was a chance she could sneak in and get him.

Two of the men, John and Jake, were continuing to drink. Chris was shooting ridiculous photos of all of them with the camera. Ryan was going through Isaak's backpack, tossing things out as he went.

A big smile spread across Ryan's face when he pulled out the satellite phone. He held it in the air for Isaak to see. "Look what we have here."

Dani let out a small sigh and whispered to herself. "Crap. I knew I should have put that in my bag."

Ryan taunted Isaak. "You're not going to need this anymore." Ryan put the phone on the ground. He used the butt of his rifle to smash it. Ryan then turned and faced his buddies. He threw his arm out. "Who packed the whiskey?"

At this point, Dani knew it would be a waiting game. These men were definitely feeling their oats. From the empty cans and bottles littering their camp, they had drunk enough to knock out an elephant. She just had to bide her time. When they were all asleep, that would be when she would put her plan into action. It wasn't the world's best plan, but it was all she had right now. She would sneak into the camp and do her best to untie Isaak and retrieve their things before anyone noticed. A long shot at best.

That was going to be a difficult task, but she wasn't going to let a little fear keep her from helping

Isaak. After all, this was all her fault. While she waited, she would continue to mentally flog herself for leading Isaak into this situation.

This was highly unprofessional on her part, and this was certainly not what his boss had signed him up for by any means. Why had she thought it was alright to make him trek through the woods to save that bear? It wasn't his job to do that. Dani had just gotten ahead of herself, not to mention she had grown too accustomed to his company. She trusted him, which wasn't an easy task for her to do.

Shaking off her thoughts, she sat there waiting for the hunters to fall asleep. By the time they did, she was pretty sure her feet were frozen asleep. The four poachers inside the camp had finally into a drunken slumber. The one who had captured Isaak had a half-empty bottle of whiskey cradled in his arms. The fire had burned low, and only the glowing embers gave off light. Dani's eyes were accustomed to the darkness, and her feet were sure in their steps as she made her way into the camp.

Isaak was still awake. He saw her tiptoe into camp, and his eyes grew wide as if to tell her to get the hell out of there. Fat chance. No way was she going to leave him here. She put her finger to her lips, cautioning Isaak to keep quiet. She picked up Isaak's backpack and carefully moved the camera out from beneath Chris's hand. With a loud snore, Chris rolled over and continued to sleep. Dani put the camera strap around her neck. Sneaking back out of camp, she deposited the items next to her backpack on the ground.

With her knife in hand, she hid behind the tree Isaak was tied to and started sawing through the ropes. Dani nudged his shoulder, and with a nod of her head, she tried to communicate their need to evacuate the area as soon as possible. They just might make it out of this alive if they were quieter than the caterpillars that crawled on the leaves.

Isaak stood up and nodded his head toward the poachers. Dani motioned with her hand to come on. She had no idea what he was trying to do, but there was absolutely no reason to get any closer to those fools. It was time to put as much distance between them as possible.

Isaak shook his head no and headed into the camp. He crawled quietly over to Jake. When he got close enough, his fingers inched up toward Jake's shirt pocket. Isaak reached in carefully and retrieved his cell phone. Then he moved quietly away from the poachers and joined Dani on the outskirts of the camp. When he did, his arms wrapped around Dani in a fierce hug that she couldn't help but return.

Dani laid her head on his shoulder for a brief second before whispering to him. "There's no time for this. We have to get away from here."

"Okay," Isaak whispered as he reluctantly released her.

They each grabbed their gear and tiptoed away from the camp. When they were far enough away, they moved faster. Dani led him in the same direction as the wounded bear, hoping to make it to the injured animal before the poachers did. It was on the way to their meetup point too, so it would serve two purposes. They would need to make up for the lost time if they were going to get to their ride in time.

Dani lost track of how long they walked through the night. At some point, they had to sit down to take a small rest. She set her alarm, so they didn't sleep too long. While the hunters were drunk, they wouldn't sleep forever, and when they found that Isaak was missing, they would hightail it out of their camp and come searching for them. Whether they were skilled enough to catch their tracks was another thing. Dani would have been able to, but her father had taught her how. It was a skill her people had passed down from one generation to the next, and it had always come in handy.

When the phone alarm pealed, they both had jolted awake faster than usual. The forest was quiet as the first rays of the morning shone through the trees. Dani and Isaak quickly finished their morning routines before they packed their gear and were ready to move on.

Isaak reached into his backpack and pulled out two protein bars. He tossed one to Dani, who reluctantly caught it. "Eat, Dani."

"I'm not hungry." Dani scanned the surrounding area, looking for any sign of the hunters. In theory, they were probably passed out drunk, but they could have strong constitutions. Their hangovers might not be enough to keep them from moving.

"Damn it, Dani. The bear can wait. Eat."

"It's not the bear I'm worried about, Isaak."

"They were pretty drunk when we left. It's not likely they'll feel well enough to run a marathon first thing. What makes you think they'll come after us?"

"You're not from here, Isaak. You wouldn't understand." Dani pointed to the camera. "In their minds, you might be instrumental in getting them caught. You've seen them, and you have pictures. You're a threat."

Isaak opened his phone and tried to get a signal. "Still nothing."

"I wish they hadn't destroyed the satellite phone." If they still had the satellite phone, Dani could have already called in reinforcements. Now they might be sitting ducks. A hangover might slow them down, but it certainly wouldn't stop them from pursuing Isaak. Dani shuddered at the thought.

"You still want to track this bear?"

"I have to see this through. I know you don't understand." Dani knew he probably never would.

Isaak turned away from her and stared off into the distance. "No, I think I do. There's nothing you wouldn't do to protect what you care about."

"Like you did?" added Dani.

Isaak turned back to look at her. "But I didn't. If anything, I put us more at risk."

"Isaak...." Dani reached out to touch his arm, but Isaak pulled away.

"You're right. We should keep moving." Isaak stood up and moved further away from her.

"You're being too hard on yourself, Isaak." She understood his guilt. Dani felt the same thing deep inside. He had been put at risk because of her. Dani would probably never forgive herself for that. All she could do now was make sure he survived this ordeal.

"Am I? I should be the one rescuing you." He clenched his right fist.

"Why? Because you're the man? I didn't take you for a man with an ego." She felt her ire rising. Dani thought he was different. He hadn't second guessed her ability to lead him through the forest, not like some of the other men. Had he just pretended?

"You didn't?" Isaak looked at her suspiciously.

"Okay, maybe in the beginning." Her smile was teasing.

"And now?"

Dani held up her thumb and forefinger about an inch or so apart. "Just a little bit. Just so we're clear, though, you saved me too."

Isaak waved her words away. "It all happened so fast."

"Yet you made it a point to keep me safe," Dani pointed out.

Isaak grinned. "I'm not sure anyone else would have seen it that way. Dumb luck, really."

"I don't suppose you'll be giving us a five-star rating." Dani wouldn't blame him in the least.

"Are you kidding? How many wildlife tours have such harrowing adventures?"

"You'd be surprised." Dani picked up the protein bar and opened the wrapper. Her stomach almost growled its approval. She was hungry, but her brain was telling her that they needed to move more than they needed to shove food into their mouths.

Isaak scanned the distance. "Do you think the bear's still alive?"

"If not, there will be proof." Dani wasn't looking forward to finding a dead bear. A wounded one was bad enough, but the dead ones made her feel helpless.

She always imagined how terrified they must feel in their final hours. Not to mention the pain and not knowing what caused it. They should be able to live in a world where they don't have to fear being hunted in their natural habitat.

"And if we do find it, how will we alert the proper channels?" asked Isaak. He opened his phone again and shook his head when he found no bars.

"We'll figure something out." It was a hollow promise. They would need a miracle at this point. She wasn't sure she believed in those anymore.

Chapter 13

Back at the camp, the hunters were still sleeping. The four of them were sprawled out in various positions. Some sprawled out on the ground in their sleeping bags. Some had passed out in their chairs and hadn't moved an inch. None of them knew that their prisoner was no longer there, but they were sure about to find out.

Ryan was the first one to show signs of life as he awoke with a slight groan. He put his hand to his head, and his eyes slowly opened. He squinted as the sun hit his eyes. A flash of pain crossed his features. "Damn whiskey."

He sat up slowly and blinked a few times as he

tried to come fully awake. Glancing around the camp at his comrades, he surveyed the area. When his eyes touched on the tree where Isaak should have been, his expression changed to anger. "Son of a!"

John grumbled on the ground next to him and rolled over to get more comfortable. "Not so loud."

"He's gone," growled Ryan.

Jake opened his eyes and let out a huge yawn as he slowly rose to a sitting position. "Who's gone?"

"Bigfoot. Who do ya think? Who was watching him?" asked Ryan.

John's eyes flew open in alarm. He sat up suddenly and grabbed his head. His face screwed up in pain. "Aahh, that hurts. I thought Chris was."

Ryan threw the half-empty whiskey bottle on the ground near Chris. It shattered, jolting Chris awake. The man scrambled to a sitting position, confused. "Hey! What'd you do that for? That was perfectly good whiskey."

"Where did he go?" Ryan demanded.

"Where did who go?" Chris was confused.

"I'm surrounded by idiots," muttered Ryan.

Chris glanced over at Jake, who gestured to the

ropes lying on the ground next to the tree where Isaak had been tied before. Realization finally hit Chris. "Shit!"

"Did you delete the photos?" asked Ryan.

"Which ones?" asked Chris.

"The ones you took of all of us last night." Jake rubbed his head with his fingers.

Chris looked to the ground, guilty. "I was going to," mumbled Chris.

"Damn it! So not only does he know what we were up to, he has our first names and pictures of each of us to prove it." Ryan kicked the dirt with his foot. He almost looked like a toddler throwing a tantrum.

"What are we gonna do?" asked John.

"What do you mean what are we gonna do? Get them back, dipshit. I'm surrounded by idiots. Pack up. We're moving out," ordered Ryan.

"What are we going to do when we find him this time?" Jake asked.

"Something he's not likely to get out of." Ryan's face was full-on determined this time.

Jake, John, and Chris exchanged quiet glances as they took in Ryan's words. None of them looked prepared to execute another human being, but none of them would go against Ryan. They never had. He was always their leader, and he had a wicked streak that scared the hell out of the rest of them.

~*~

As the early morning hours passed into mid-morning, Isaak and Dani had put quite some distance between themselves and the poacher's camp. Isaak was starting to feel a little less worried about the men who had held him captive. Just a little. He was sure he would remember that moment for the rest of his life. Is that what it felt like to be carjacked? Isaak imagined it was relatively close. Some might be exhilarated by the experience. Maybe he would later, but right now, he was too close to the heart of it. Not to mention he was worried about what would happen when they did track down the bear.

What were they going to do if they found it alive? He was fairly certain that Dani wasn't trained in veterinary sciences. But then again, they hadn't exactly exchanged their full life stories. Why should they? It wasn't like this trip was some kind of romantic rendezvous. He didn't really believe in them. Or he hadn't. Isaak could almost see himself camping out with Dani somewhere else, but with a little more camping gear than they had brought along, and that wasn't something he had ever imagined himself doing before. Being with her made him think about the world in different ways.

These were thoughts that a self-confirmed bachelor didn't need to be having. They were not far from finishing their week. All they had to do was survive the next day or so, and then Isaak would return back to the city, his natural habitat. That thought didn't make him as happy as he thought it would. He should feel relieved, and yet it made him feel just a little empty.

They were now coming to the top of a hill, which gave them a better vantage point. The hill overlooked a lush meadow below. Further down the incline was another heavily forested area with trees as far as the eyes could see. As Isaak took it in, he almost missed the raven flying overhead. He nearly jumped when he saw the shadow it cast on the ground near them.

Dani put her hand over her eyes and scanned the skies. "Follow him."

"Is he going to lead us to the bear?" Isaak would

have to see it before he believed it. Then again, stranger things had been known to happen. It was the raven that clued them into the injured bear in the first place. He started to think that Dani was an animal whisperer. Was there anything she couldn't do? Yes, live in his concrete jungle.

"Have a little faith," she reassured him.

Isaak shrugged. "I guess it couldn't hurt."

"That's the spirit." Dani smiled at him, then turned to see the bird land on a tree further down the hill.

"Caw!" called the bird.

"Do you think he found something?" wondered Dani.

"That or he's just messing with me again." Isaak shrugged again. Damned if he knew what the bird was up to. If he had been a city bird, the raven would be scouting for food. They were quite used to people dropping food and other debris. Humans were the worst when it came to caring for the world around them. Isaak wasn't innocent himself, but he was determined to do better after this trip.

A loud roar erupted, sending the bird up from

his perch. Dani turned to look at Isaak with an 'I told you so smile,' and he cut her off at the pass. "Don't even say it."

"I wasn't." Dani feigned innocence.

"Now what?" asked Isaak. He was actually afraid of her answer.

"We'll get a closer look." Dani nodded to where the sound of the roaring animal had come. As if to punctuate its presence, the beast roared again.

That's what he was afraid of. "Is that wise?" It seemed like heading into a dragon's den to him. Nothing good was going to come of this. Okay, maybe something good could come of it, but Isaak was not really wanting to see what that was. In his mind, he saw the bear gobbling him up like turkey dinner.

Danni smirked at him. "Do you really want me to answer that?"

Isaak shook his head and sighed deeply. "Not really." He knew better at this point. He also knew there would be no stopping Dani. She was too pigheaded and strong-willed to talk any sense into. He would just have to go with the flow and hope they both made it out of this in one piece.

Chapter 14

The four poachers were walking through the forest. It was unsurprising that Ryan was in the lead. Chris was behind him, with Jake and John holding up the rear as they walked side by side.

"How do we even know they went this way?" whispered Jake.

"Don't look at me. He's the one who seems to know everything," replied John in a soft voice.

Ryan turned at their words, but the two of them looked away and pretended to be minding their own business. Neither one of them wanted to gain Ryan's attention. Their leader was far past cranky at this point. He was almost homicidal. No one wanted to push any of his buttons, and when he stopped abruptly and bent down to look at the ground, the others followed suit.

"What do you see?" asked Chris.

"This here is a shoe print." Ryan pointed out a fresh footprint in the mud. "I'm willing to bet it's our man."

"What about that one?" Chris pointed to a smaller pair of footprints.

"Looks like we're lookin' for a man and woman," concluded John.

"Or a man and one the size of Jake," added Chris.

Jake scowled at Chris. "You callin' me a woman?"

"If the shoe fits." Chris shrugged.

"Shut up! All of ya," roared Ryan. "Keep movin'. We still got ground to cover."

Ryan stood up and started moving ahead. His face was set in stone. His body was rigid as he walked forward with determined strides. No one wanted to run afoul of him right now.

"This is the last time I go into the woods with any of you," complained John.

"You always say that, and yet here you are," Jake pointed out.

Ryan took just enough time to glare menacingly at his group. It was the 'shut your pie hole' look. Everyone read its meaning and stopped their idle chatter. Once again, they went back to tracking the two people who could get them sent to lock up if they made it out of the woods before the hunters found them.

~*~

As Isaak and Dani continued down the hill, they could hear the bear getting louder. Isaak could see a large mass of black fur behind a tree. He was not looking forward to whatever came next. He was fairly sure it would involve him passing out or running away screaming like a banshee.

As they made their way closer to the tree, Dani cautioned him. "Careful."

Isaak held up his hands and shook his head. "You don't have to tell me twice."

Dani motioned for him to follow her. "I need to get a little closer."

"Of course you do." His voice was sarcastic, but he still managed to have a small grin on his face.

Isaak followed close behind her. He didn't like the idea of her getting too close, either. Wounded animals, they were extremely unpredictable. He'd watched enough Animal Planet to know that for sure. "Be careful."

The two of them edged slowly closer until they were about ten feet away from the bear. Isaak didn't feel any better being this close to it. Just because it was laying still didn't mean it wasn't ready to attack them at a moment's notice. The two of them crouched to get a better view through the leaves. The bear was laying on its side. Painful grunts could be heard amidst heavy breathing. Its fur was matted near the hind legs, where Isaak assumed the wound was still fresh.

The sound of buzzing interrupted the stillness, and the bear's head turned to look over to where they were behind the trees. Dani gave him an incredulous look, speaking without thinking. "Would you turn that thing off?"

Isaak pulled the phone out of his pocket and looked at the screen. A text from his mother scrolled across the screen. Then he saw the two bars on the top of his screen. "I've got bars."

Dani and Isaak's eyes met, and relief crossed over her face. "Hand it here. I know just who to call.

The park ranger will be able to send help."

Isaak handed the phone to Dani. "Better be quick. Before it changes its mind."

Dani dialed the park ranger's office and put the cell phone on speaker. The call went through, and the Ranger on the other end answered. "This is Ranger Daniels. How can I help you?"

"Ty! It's Dani."

"Dani. What can I help you with?" asked Ty.

"We're in a little situation here at Great Bear," she continued.

"Go on," said Tyler

"I have an injured grisly out here. It's still alive, but some poachers have really messed it up."

Isaak watched Dani pace while she filled Tyler in on the situation. He wished he could feel relieved that they were able to get ahold of someone. That's what he should feel. Deep inside, though, he felt regret. It meant their time was coming to an end. As dangerous as this adventure had become, it was still an adventure with a woman who more than captivated him. He wanted to know more about her, what made her tick and if she felt the same pull he did.

"Have you come into contact with them?" asked Tyler.

"Yes. Four of them tied Isaak up when he was caught spying on them, but I managed to get him free," she explained.

Thanks for that. Isaak fought the urge to sulk. Way to make him sound like a completely useless fool. The man would probably be laughing at him all the way here and possibly most of the way to his headquarters, wherever that may be.

"Of course you did. Never was smart enough to stay away from the fight," chastised the ranger.

"You know me. Protecting these lands is in my blood." Dani was actually grinning like the cat that got into the cream.

Isaak had the distinct impression that these two had been more than friends at some point. Once transplanted in his brain, that idea took root and blossomed into full-blown loathing for the man on the phone. That ranger was going to come to save them, and all he could think about was how much he already hated the man.

"Where are the poachers now?" asked Tyler.

"I'm not sure. We left them drunk in their camp several miles away from here. Can you ping my location?"

"I'll do my best. Stay where you are, Dani. We'll come to get you," answered Tyler.

"And if they come first?" asked Dani.

Now why in the hell did she have to ask that? Isaak wasn't even trying to go there in his head. Dani was already six moves ahead. Shoot. She was probably imagining what would happen if the hunters came at them with their guns blazing right now. Isaak didn't suffer those fantasies. He refused to have them.

"Stay out of sight," warned the ranger.

"We'll do our best. Just hurry up. The bear's still breathing, but it's in a lot of pain."

"Don't worry. I'll bring backup," added Tyler.

Dani disconnected the call and handed the phone back to Isaak. "Here. Make sure you keep it on, so they can track our position."

Isaak nodded at her. "How long will it take them?"

"I don't know. We need to stay put so they can get to us." Dani looked over her shoulder and searched through the trees behind them.

Isaak did the same. Now that she had put the thought in his head, he was also wondering what they would do if the poachers showed their ugly faces. "And if those guys get to us first?"

"I'll be waiting for them." Dani reached into her bag and pulled out a small handgun.

Isaak thought he was losing his mind. She had a gun, a real gun. "Has that been there this whole time?"

"Relax, the safety is on."

Safety. The safety? Is that what she really thought this was about? Not at all. How in the hell could she have had that in there the whole time? "You could have used that at any time."

Dani gave him a placating smile. "Yes, but they had the advantage."

"And how is now any different? There's still four of them." Four to two, and only one of them had a weapon to use. Isaak was not a gun man. Hell, he'd never even held one before. Unlike most black stereotypes, not all dark-skinned people had a gun hidden in the back of their pants.

"Yes, but they only know about two of us,"

added Dani.

Two? Like he was even remotely useful. It was more like one and a half. The only thing he had managed to do was not give away her presence. "Two? You already saw how useless I was."

Dani smiled at him. "I thought you were brave."

"Oh?" Isaak's eyebrow rose, and a slow smile broadened his face.

"I'm sorry I brought you into this mess." Her face started to cloud with regret.

Isaak turned to look at the tortured animal laying on the ground. Then he looked back at her with a serious look on his face. "I'm not."

It was the truth. Deep down, he knew there was a greater lesson at play here. It wasn't just how to survive in the wild. It was how to do so without destroying it. How in the world could he tell his readers that without alienating them from their own hobbies? How many of their readers hunted for sport? This would definitely be something he would need to research before he tackled his article. That was if they did indeed manage to make it out of this situation alive.

"You should get some rest," suggested Dani.

"What are you going to do?" he asked her.

"Keep a lookout." Dani was already scanning the horizon with a determined look on her face.

"Okay, but if something happens, you better wake me up." Isaak could use just a little cat nap if he was going to keep his wits about him.

"I will," promised Dani.

Isaak glanced back at the bear. "And don't let him eat me."

"Got it." Dani shook her head and rolled her eyes at the grinning man. She put her backpack against the tree and leaned against it. Her eyes trained on the forest behind them.

Isaak set his pack against the tree and laid down, so his head was resting on it. He placed the cell phone on the ground next to him and folded his hands over his stomach. He shut his eyes and tried to get his thoughts to quiet down long enough to get a little sleep.

~*~

The ranger's office was a small wooden structure set in a clearing. Four large ATVs were parked out front. A pole barn structure was near the office building. Under the roof of the pole barn were two trailers and two additional ATVs. The rangers used them to monitor the environmental safety of the Great Bear Rainforest as well as the physical well-being of the animals that took shelter within the forest. Conservation and preservation worked hand in hand here. All the rangers had sworn to protect and serve in their roles, and today was no different.

Two park rangers, Emma and Will, were running from the pole barn, pulling a flatbed ATV trailer behind them. They were hooking it up to the back of one of the 4 wheelers when Tyler and another ranger, Charlie, exited the building. Charlie was holding an electronic GPS in his hands.

Tyler pointed back toward the office. "Emma, don't forget the medical kit."

"On it." Emma trotted back into the building.

"Will, are the ATVs ready?" asked Tyler.

"They're full of fuel. Mine has two more gas cans secured if we need them," answered Will.

Tyler turned to Charlie, who was concentrating on the GPS. "Charlie, what's our ETA?"

Charlie's eyes turned to the woods, then back at Tyler. "Baring that there are no felled trees in our way, our ETA should be about an hour."

Tyler frowned, then boarded his ATV. "Dani may not have an hour."

Emma ran out of the building with the medical bag slung across her shoulders. "Medical kit's ready."

Tyler started his ATV and shouted his orders. "Load up! Let's ride!"

Chapter 15

The four poachers were walking through the forest, which was now leading up to the hill. None of them spoke, for they were afraid of Ryan's wrath, which seemed to be greater the further they traveled. They had been walking all morning with empty stomachs and pounding heads. Ryan barely even let them stop for a pit stop. He was a taskmaster, prepared to push them well past their limits.

Ryan held his hand up as they neared the hill. "Stop!"

A small roar could be heard in the distance. Each man had a different reaction. One gleeful smile, and the rest three different shades of terror. While they had felled the beast, they were actually hoping he would already be dead by the time they caught up to him.

"That the bear?" asked John.

"Sounds like it," answered Ryan.

"You reckon they found it?" Jake's voice made him sound like he was hoping that the people they were tracking were long gone, even though they had the capacity to change the course of his life.

"Only one way to find out," said Ryan.

"What if there's more than two of them? I don't think this is a good idea." Chris had a hollow look on his face.

Ryan held his rifle up. "We got plenty of back up right here. Now quit your bitchin' and get your head in the game."

The four of them continued slowly, taking their time as they perused the area with every step they took. They could hear the injured bear wailing in the background. Soon, they would put it out of its misery. Then they would skin it, take the gallbladder, and leave the rest of it there for the other animals to scavenge. The fur and gallbladder were the only things they were interested in. Some poachers used the whole animal. A full stuffed bear could go for a lot of money, but this excursion had already been a little too close for comfort. It was time to shorten the load.

~*~

Time passed slowly as Dani kept watch. She saw the raven fly overhead again. It came from up the hillside and called down while in flight. Dani felt its message to the core. Danger. Panic rose quickly, and she called over to Isaak. "Get up, Isaak."

Isaak's eyes flew open upon hearing her words, and he rose to a sitting position. "The ranger?"

"Don't know, but I've got a bad feeling." And that feeling was multiplying by the second. This was definitely going down in her top three most memorable trips. She only hoped they made it out of here alive.

"What do you want me to do?" Isaak looked down the hill and saw a faint trace of movement.

"Get behind that tree." Dani gestured to the tree that had wider coverage. It just so happened that the tree was four feet closer to the bear that was still wide awake and mad as hell that it couldn't get back up on its feet.

This fact was not lost on Isaak. "But what if the

bear attacks us?"

"Do you trust me?"

Isaak and Dani locked eyes, and the two shared a brief moment before Isaak replied. "I trust you, Dani."

Isaak stopped to pick up his pack and moved from his spot. The bear lifted its head to look at him and bared its fangs threateningly. "Easy...easy. Don't eat me."

The bear put its head down and let out a huff of air through its nose before making a louder snorting sound. Dani was watching every second. "Now you're talking to him?"

Isaak grinned at her remark. "I'll do a tap dance if it keeps him from killing me."

Dani's eyes darted to the movement at the bottom of the hill. She whispered to Isaak. "Quiet!"

Dani could see the hunters moving in from the bottom of the hill. They weren't being quiet by any means. It was almost like they wanted them to hear them. This was just a big game to them. It was when they pointed their guns in their direction that made her feel ice cold.

A loud crack interrupted the silence. A bullet hit

the tree behind Isaak's head. The bark flew off it and landed on the ground at his feet. Both Dani and Isaak dove to the ground. Isaak was the first to speak. "Those idiots nearly got us."

Dani nodded to the left. "Isaak, we need to go, now! We don't have time to wait for help."

Isaak grabbed his cell phone and shoved it into his pocket. "What about the bear?"

Dani glanced at the bear. She didn't want to leave the bear, but they would be no help to it if they were dead. There was only one thing to do, try to lead them away and stay alive in the process. "We'll lead them away from the bear."

Isaak and Dani ran through the trees. Dani had her gun in her hand, ready to use it if the need arose. She'd never fired it at another human before, but there was a first time for everything. When she turned around to take another look, she could see the poachers making their way down the hill. It looked like they were heading in their direction. The new course they were taking was away from the bear. That meant the bear might be safe for the time being.

Another shot rang out, and a bullet hit the ground

just in front of Isaak. Dust flew as the bullet embedded into the earth. Muffled shouts could be heard in the distance, but Dani and Isaak pressed on, running as fast as their legs would carry them.

~*~

The rangers pulled into a clearing. They stopped to check the coordinates to make sure they were heading in the right direction. Tyler turned to Charlie. "Update?"

"Tyler, we're about five minutes out, but they're on the move heading West."

"Shit! The poachers must have found them." Tyler slapped the steering wheel. He looked over his shoulder at Emma and Will. "We need to move! Now!"

The 4 wheelers took off again. The urgency was palpable. They all considered Dani part of their ranger family. She had done so much to help them patrol the area when she was on her adventures through the forest. Dani knew the heartbeat of every area of the forest.

They flew through the forest, trying to make up the distance as quickly as possible. The fact that Dani was still moving was a good sign. Unless the poachers had taken the phone from her. That was a possibility, but in that case, they would at least be able to catch the culprits.

When they heard a distant boom, Tyler stopped his ATV and pulled over. He gestured to the others to do the same. "Shots fired."

Charlie nodded. "Sounds like they aren't too far now."

"We'll leave the ATVs here. Sneak up from behind." Tyler was the first to hop off his vehicle. He retrieved his gun and pointed to the top of the hill. "Draw your weapons, and be careful."

~*~

The four poachers broke through the tree line to begin their descent. Chris pointed across the meadow to where Isaak and Dani were running. "There!"

Ryan took aim with the rifle and was about to shoot when a loud boom exploded nearby. A bullet ricocheted off the bark of the tree behind the hunters. All four of them ducked.

"They're armed!" shouted Jake.

"So are we, you idiot," growled Ryan.

"Where'd that journalist get the gun?" asked John.

"'Spect that woman of his had it," Ryan speculated.

"What are we gonna do?" asked Chris.

They all looked to Ryan, who clenched his jaw."Kill 'em."

Ryan stood up to fire the rifle. Another shot fired, and Ryan dove for cover as bark flew from another tree. That didn't keep him from firing off a shot of his own when he hit the ground. Two could play that game.

~*~

Dani and Isaak were each hiding behind a tree when Ryan's shot nearly took out Dani's head. A little more to the right, and she would have been a goner. Isaak was glad that the man had missed. He wasn't prepared to sit here and watch her die.

"That one was close." Isaak checked her for any visible wounds.

Dani glanced at the mark left on the tree, then turned and aimed her handgun. Click! Dani closed her eyes and hung her head. "The clip's empty."

Well, that was not good news. Isaak wondered what they were going to do now. He didn't want to imagine his life flashing before his eyes, but what choice did he have right now?

"Should we keep moving?" he asked her.

"I'm not sure it will do much good. They'd know every step we made at this point." Dani was deflated.

This was the first time Isaak had seen her this way. She had been strong and extremely able this whole time. This was the first time he had seen any of her cracks. Isaak felt the need to protect her fire up inside him. He reached over and touched her cheek with his fingertips. "We're going to make it out of this, Dani."

Dani leaned her face into his hand and closed her eyes. Isaak pulled her to him and held her.

~*~

The poachers were crouched down together. They were keeping an eye on their targets.

"They didn't return fire," said John.

"They're out of bullets." An evil grin crossed Ryan's face. Ryan stood up and motioned for the others to do the same. The other three rose to their feet. "Let's go finish this."

The sound of a hammer engaging on a gun clicked behind them as the ranger Tyler Daniels made his presence known. "Put the rifle down! Now!"

The four poachers froze in place, and the ranger continued with his orders. "Do it now! No sudden movements."

Ryan lowered the rifle to the ground. "You're makin' a mistake, officer. We ain't done nothin'."

"Put your hands in the air, and don't move," ordered Tyler. Tyler nodded to his comrades. "Cuff 'em."

As the other rangers stepped forward and cuffed the poachers, Tyler began to read them their rights. "You have the right to remain silent...."

~*~

Isaak looked around the tree he was behind up to the top of the hill. He was surprised that he couldn't hear the firing anymore. "They've stopped firing."

Dani glanced around her tree and smiled. "Reinforcements have arrived."

Dani stood up and started to move toward the rangers who had taken care of their attackers. Isaak followed her, thankful that the cavalry had come just in time. He'd never doubt her again. She had been a force the whole time, one that believed that help would come at just the right time. Isaak was starting to think the universe spoke to her in ways he would never even begin to understand. It was a talent he would never have, even if he tried to live his days somewhere outside of the city.

When they made it down to the meadow below the hill, they found that the rangers had the poachers cuffed and well under control. Isaak nodded to the rangers when they looked up to see them approaching. He didn't know what else to do. How did you thank someone for saving your life without looking like a fool? Every word that wanted to come out of his mouth right now was weak and lacked any sense of confidence. A close brush with death could do that to him, not to mention it was his second close brush in two days. If he never saw those poachers again, he would be one happy man.

Dani walked up to Tyler, smiling. "Great to see you, Ty. You made good time. Thank you."

Tyler and Dani fist-bumped before Tyler greeted her in return. "I'm glad we were in time. I heard the gunshots and thought we might be too late."

Isaak stepped forward.

"Tyler, I'd like you to meet Isaak Lee."

Tyler reached out to shake Isaak's hand. "It's nice to meet you, Isaak. Any friend of Dani's is a friend of mine."

"So, what happens now?" asked Isaak.

Tyler gestured to the poachers. "These four will be going to jail. Emma's not sure if the bear will make it or not. I've radioed this in. A chopper will be here shortly to take these four to jail. Can I count on you two to testify?"

"You know you can always count on me." Dani nodded her agreement right away.

"Count me in too." Isaak handed Tyler the memory card from his camera. "Here are the pictures I took. Those idiots took a bunch of their own pictures. They're here too. All I ask is that you email the rest of the photos to me. Most of my trip is on that memory card. I need those photos for my story. I brought another memory card for the rest of my trip."

"Thanks. I'll be happy to."

Tyler reached into his pocket, retrieved Isaac's wallet, and handed it to him. "Here. I believe this is yours."

Isaak smiled and reached for his wallet. "Thanks."

Tyler glanced back at Dani. "Do you two need a lift back to civilization?"

Dani shook her head. "No, but thanks. I promised Isaak I'd show him my favorite spot before we ended his trip. You could do us a favor, though."

"I'll do my best," answered Tyler.

Dani glanced at Isaak, then turned back to Tyler. "Ty, may I speak to you in private?"

Tyler smiled. "Sure."

Isaak frowned as Dani walked away with Tyler. Both of them were talking too low for him to hear. He wasn't too keen on being left in the dark, but he had learned to trust her with his life. More than likely, their conversation had nothing to do with him anyway.

Chapter 16

Through the canopy of the trees above, the blue sky was slightly tinged with the hint of a few billowy clouds. Soft light filtered through the trees, making glowing dots on the ground around them that reminded Dani of sequins dancing in the light. Now that they were alone again and no longer under the fear of hunters, Dani had started to relax in Isaak's company. In fact, when their fingers had brushed, Dani let her hand link with his. They were still walking together, hand in hand, enjoying the silence as they trekked through the woods.

The fight or flight syndrome had left, and she was starting to feel more like herself, except for one little thing. Her need to shove every handsome man away from her to protect herself had seemed to evaporate completely. Dani wanted to pull Isaak closer, but she didn't know how to voice that need. It seemed like a weakness, one that made her feel uncomfortable. Most of the time, she was confident in her own shoes, walking tall and proud no matter what the world threw at her. Right now, she doesn't feel confident about anything. Instead, she felt like a schoolgirl out on her first date with her first crush. Awkward? Definitely. Weak? Maybe. Confused? She had been that since the moment he first smiled at her.

What was wrong with her? She knew he would be leaving. That thought cut her to the core far deeper than she cared to admit, even to herself. Dani wouldn't admit it to anyone else anytime soon, either. She was desperate to hang onto her tough exterior. Dani tried to push those thoughts aside and enjoy these last moments with Isaak.

"We're almost there. Do you hear it?" Dani pointed to the distance.

"The rushing water? You're not planning on white water rafting, are you?" Isaak had a cautious smile on his face.

She laughed softly. "Not on this trip. Maybe another time." Dani almost clapped her hand over her mouth. What was she thinking? This was a bad idea all around. It was never a good idea to let her heart override her mind. She had learned that a long time ago. Her eyes met his, and she saw a warmth inside them that almost melted her resolve completely.

"I'd like that." He squeezed her hand.

"Me too. Although we'd have to wrap you up in bubble wrap," teased Dani.

"I'm not that fragile." Isaak took a deep breath and sighed.

Fragile? No, he was right. He was far from it. Courageous, caring, determined, handsome, gentle, and a whole lot more. She needed more time to uncover all his charming attributes. "No, you're not."

"Caw!" The raven made his presence known. Dani and Isaak both looked up to see where the bird had landed.

"You again?" Isaak closed one eye and glared up at the bird with his other.

"I think he likes you." Dani had never seen

the raven take to an outsider like this. She had seen them many times in the rainforest. Dani had always considered them feathered friends, fellow explorers like herself. Maybe they saw the same in Isaak. It was something she was sure he had never seen in himself before. It certainly wasn't a natural occurrence for a city slicker. Dani couldn't remember any other patrons who would have survived this experience.

"He's kind of grown on me too, but if he shows up in Toronto, I'm calling you to retrieve him," added Isaak.

"You want me to come to Toronto?" Dani was surprised he mentioned that. It intrigued her yet terrified her at the same time. She feared he would end up just like Jason if she started a real relationship with him. Visiting him could turn into him pressuring her to leave her world behind and assimilate into his. That was the worst-case scenario, one that she didn't have to imagine just yet. Dani had to learn to live in the moment instead of preplanning the future with the fantasies she had in her head. Not every fantasy was a good one. Sometimes a fantasy was a self-fulfilling prophecy. If she imagined him only leaving her in the end, she would set a whole course in their relationship that would cultivate that fantasy, all based on her own paranoia.

Isaak shrugged his shoulders, unaware of her thoughts. "If you wanted to. I could show you how we rough it in the concrete jungle."

"I'm sure it's a primitive life," teased Dani.

"I mean it, though."

"Let's talk about it later, Isaak. For now, can we just stay in this moment?" Dani was sure he meant it and knew he didn't know how patronizing it sounded. There was bending a little and caving in completely. She needed him to be the kind of man that didn't want her to give up her life or change her circumstances to make a relationship work.

Dani squeezed his hand and started to pull him faster through the woods, suddenly ready to change the subject completely. "Come on!"

"Someone's impatient," teased Isaak.

Dani ignored him and continued to lead him through the forest until they started down a small trail. The flat trail led to a large viewing platform near the edge of a cliff, one that Dani had visited many times.

It was just across from a waterfall that cascaded from the Brandywine Creek. The free-falling water splashed down below, churning into frothy white waves. Dani turned to look at Isaak's face and was happy to see him watching the view with great interest.

Isaak released her hand and reached for his camera. He started to take photos of the waterfall from every angle. Every few clicks, he dropped his camera and just took in the view. It was not a giant waterfall, not Niagara sized in the least, but large enough to send a spray of mist back into their faces.

As Isaak continued to take pictures, Dani started to scan the shore not far from the base of the falls. Every time she came here, there were all kinds of wildlife nearby. The water meant life for the earth below and the animals that made this area their home. Water was sustenance, a rejuvenation in many ways. Every time she came here, Dani felt like her burdens were lifted for a short time. The world spun a little slower, and she could tackle her problems one at a time. Today, she didn't have any burdens, just a need for Isaak to see her heart without actually having to say a word. This place was everything she loved about her world and why she would never give it up.

As she continued scouting the area, something miraculous happened. A small white spirit bear cub was moving into view, followed closely by a large black kermode bear. The cub started dipping its paw into the water and cleaning its face. Its mother stood beside it and lifted her face up to sniff the air. When the mama bear smelled their presence, it started to make slow chuffing sounds.

"Isaak...." whispered Dani.

Isaak turned to her and whispered, "Why are we whispering?"

"Look...." Dani gestured to the water below, and Isaak's eyes followed.

Isaak's eyes grew wide. "Is that a...."

"Shhh...not so loud," cautioned Dani.

"Well, I'll be." Isaak started to snap photos of the cub with its mother. It was a once in a lifetime opportunity, so it was no surprise that he would want to take it in as much as possible.

Dani continued to look down at the bears, taking in the moment. She had seen a spirit bear twice before, but never so young and innocent. It was truly a remarkable sight. "They're beautiful."

"Yes...beautiful."

Dani turned to look over at Isaak, expecting him to be looking down at the cubs. Instead, she found him looking at her with a look that made her feel like she was the most important part of the universe. She couldn't remember the last time someone had looked at her like that. As she stood there, he closed the gap between them. Before she knew it, their lips were locked in a kiss that made all thoughts disappear from her brain. The only thing she could think about was the here in now as he wrapped his arms around her back and pulled her closer to his body.

"Caw!" interrupted their favorite intruder.

They broke the kiss, and Isaak looked up at the trees. This time two ravens were sitting on the branch above. They were close together, almost beak to beak. Isaak shook his finger at the birds. "So, there was more than one of them."

"Apparently." Dani wasn't surprised, really. It made sense that the two of them would work together to cover more distance.

"I think I can see why they are so popular."

"Why's that?" She wondered where he was going with his thought process here.

"They brought us together." Isaak put a thumb on her chin and stroked it gently before kissing her softly.

Dani melted into him and let herself get lost in the moment long enough to ensure she would have the moment engraved in her memory. Then she pulled away from him, even though it was the last thing she wanted to do. "I wish we could stay here forever, but we have to get back, or we'll miss our ride."

"Would that be so bad?" Isaak looked like he was more than prepared to miss the ride if it meant spending more intimate moments with her.

Dani sighed. She would have loved to stay longer too, but there was a schedule to stick to if they were going to get out of here anytime soon. "Not if you want to walk all the way back to the beginning."

Isaak seemed to debate her words before giving in. "Point made. Let's go."

Dani and Isaak turned around to leave. He wrapped his arm around her shoulders, and the two of them started their walk back. When they made their way into a clearing, they could hear the helicopter before they could see it. The loud thwap of the blades broke through the quiet around them. Within seconds the helicopter came into view.

Isaak looked up at the helicopter. "Our ride?"

Dani smiled. "Tyler felt he owed us a favor."

Isaak shook his head in disbelief. "Really? We owe him for saving our butts."

Dani shrugged. "Lucky for us, he didn't see it that way."

They didn't talk much in the helicopter. Instead, Dani leaned up against Isaak with her head on his shoulder. It had been a long time since she had snuggled up to anyone else. Dani hadn't realized how much she had missed it. She found herself relaxing for the first time in a long time. When he reached for her hand, Dani didn't pull away. She closed her eyes as his fingers massaged her palm. The two of them just enjoyed the ride and would have enjoyed the silence had the helicopter not made an immense amount of noise. Dani tried to shut out the noise and relive the waterfall in her head as they soared over the Great Bear Rainforest.

The next hour went faster than Dani anticipated. There was a lot she could say, but the words just escaped her. Tyler gave them a ride back to her car when the helicopter touched down. Then Dani drove them back to the hotel, where each one agreed to meet up later that night when they had showered and rested a bit. It was almost like a date.

By the time Dani made her way back to the Blue Moon Bar, she had butterflies in her stomach, and she was not the kind of woman who got nervous in most situations. In this case, she had skipped her regular jeans and shirt for a dress that made her look more feminine than usual. Dani was not as comfortable in dresses. She felt like she was almost pretending to be someone else when she wore one, but tonight she decided to throw caution to the wind and just do it.

Dani was sitting at the table closest to the bar when Isaak walked through the door. He was even more handsome cleaned up than he was covered in dirt and sweat. He was wearing a long-sleeved button-up white shirt and a pair of black slacks. City wear, at least that's what she called it.

Isaak greeted her with a smile as he slid in on the

other side of the booth. "You look amazing."

"Thank you." Dani gave him a nervous smile. "So do you."

Jacob peered over the bar and greeted Isaak. He was keeping an eye on the situation like any father would. "I see she decided to keep you alive."

Isaak smiled as he turned to face her father, who was propped up on his elbows behind the bar. "She did. It was touch and go for a moment there, though."

"So I heard." Jacob exchanged a knowing look with his daughter.

Dani sighed and waited for the lecture that was sure to come. Her father was supportive of her endeavors, especially considering he had taught her everything he knew. That didn't mean he was all right with her taking on a group of poachers without decent backup. She knew she was going to hear more than an earful later. For now, she would keep that dressing down at bay for as long as possible. "Don't worry. We got 'em. That's all that matters."

"I reckon." Jacob crossed his arms over his chest and gave her a pointed glare. "Be more careful next time."

She ducked her head self-consciously. "I will," promised Dani.

Jacob cleaned a glass and snorted softly to himself before he changed the topic. "I'll bring you some hot food."

Isaak watched him disappear through the kitchen door behind the bar. "Not even going to take our order?"

"That's the way it works sometimes." Dani shrugged. "I've learned to just go with it."

Isaak reached over to clasp Dani's hand in a warm, gentle grip. "You were amazing out there."

Dani felt uneasy with the current topic. "Can we talk about something else?" She didn't want this relationship or whatever it was becoming overshadowed by their encounter with those poachers.

Isaak smiled softly and squeezed her hand. "Like you coming to visit me in Toronto?"

Dani pulled her hand from his, uncomfortable with that topic too. "It's not that simple, Isaak."

"We don't have to make it overly complicated. Just take our time and see where it goes." Isaak's expression was hopeful.

Dani let out a heavy sigh as she gazed into Isaak's eyes. She was looking for the truth in his intentions towards her. "And how much time will you spend here?" This was the question Dani had been desperate to ask but didn't know if she should. Since he had started the ball rolling on this discussion, there was no time like the present.

"I'm not sure, Dani. In theory, I could write anywhere, but that's a logistic I would have to figure out."

A ding sounded on Isaak's phone. He glanced at it and set it face up on the table. He scanned around the bar as if he were looking for something. "Where's the...."

"Restroom?" finished Dani.

"Yeah."

"The hall on the left, at the back." Dani pointed in the general direction.

"Thanks," Isaak muttered as he stood up. He seemed a little distracted. "I'll be right back."

Dani nodded at him as he left for the restroom. She almost pointed out that he had left his phone there but figured he would make it to the bathroom before he realized. Besides, she always hated having to carry her phone into the bathroom with her. She had this fear of losing it in the toilet. Once that thing touched down inside the bowl, it was no man's land, in her opinion.

Isaak's phone dinged again, and this time the text box opened. Dani was surprised he hadn't locked the screen. She could see everything, and even though she knew she shouldn't, she couldn't stop herself from reading the screen, even if it was upside down. The text was a conversation between Isaak and Angel, who appeared to be his boss. In it, the two were discussing the Spirit Bear that Angel insisted he should use in his article if he wanted to win the award for the company. Their readers would want to know where to find such a unique animal.

Dani's face was filled with a mixture of shock and outrage. She had known he took pictures, but she thought he had known not to share its location. If hunters saw there was a cub in the Great Bear Rainforest, they would be overpopulated with poachers trying to capture the cub for personal gain. Even though hunting was illegal inside the forest, it was hard to keep an eye on every inch of the forest every second of the day.

That was the whole point she was trying to make to Isaak. She had thought he understood that.

Dani scowled at the phone. "How could he?" She then reached for the phone, picked it up and started to read through the whole group of messages when another text came through from a woman named Kat. According to her text, Kat was very lonely, and so was her bed. Dani looked through her messages and saw quite a few intimate messages had been sent his way throughout the week. Dani thought he said he was not attached to anyone. Clearly, this woman seemed to think so. She suddenly felt like such a fool. One for trusting Isaak with the forest's secrets and another for believing he was telling her the truth when he said he wanted to see her more. Was he just going to make her his chick on the side? That wasn't something Dani would ever do knowingly. Thank goodness it hadn't gone too far. Although in her heart, it had already gone far enough to make her fall for him.

Dani returned the phone to his side of the table and crossed her arms over her chest. She waited for Isaak to return. If anyone accused her of jumping off the handle here, they would be wrong. This wasn't a hair-trigger reaction. It was rational, probably more rational than giving him a piece of her heart. Dani felt like a fool.

Isaak noticed her expression when he returned. "Everything okay?"

Dani narrowed her eyes and looked up at Isaak. "You tell me," she said as she pushed his phone closer to him.

Isaak looked down at the messages, then back up at her. "You went through my phone?" He appeared to be confused and hurt by her actions.

Dani knew it looked bad. It wasn't like she was trying to go through his phone. Then again, she didn't actually stop herself. Why did she suddenly feel like a jealous teenage girlfriend? Dani thought this drama had left her several years ago. Here it was again. Although, in her case, she had a reason to be suspicious. Not of Isaak, but men in general. Jason hadn't been completely honest with her. When she had refused to move to the city, he had already been looking for a new girlfriend to replace her in his life. Dani had only found out because she had accidentally answered his phone. It only took one misstep to make a person mistrust the entire world. "It popped up."

Isaak shook his head in disbelief. "That still didn't give you the right to break my privacy." His voice was quiet, but there was a hint of anger in his tone.

Dani was a little angry herself. "When were you going to tell me?"

Isaak was taken aback. "About what?"

She couldn't believe he was acting like he didn't have any secrets he was hiding. "Isaak! Don't play stupid. You know how important that bear is." Dani decided to tackle one issue at a time. In the grand scheme of things, the bear was more important than her broken heart.

He nodded. "I do, which is why I think the world should know about it," Isaak tried to explain.

"Don't you get it?" Dani was so angry that she felt herself shaking slightly. "If you share this, even more hunters will sneak into the forest. It's bad enough that they kill the grizzlies, but hunting this one is unthinkable."

"You're foreshadowing a future that might not happen."

"You can't print that." Dani crossed her arms

over her chest again.

Isaak was at a loss as to how to proceed. "It's my livelihood, Dani. I've worked my entire life for an opportunity like this." He was trapped in a place no man wanted to be.

That's not the answer she wanted to hear. "Then you're not the man I thought you were." Dani uncrossed her arms and played with the napkin on the table.

She saw the hurt in his expression but didn't let it sway her as he continued. "I'm still the same man, Dani. I'm not going to write anything to put them at risk." Isaak tried to reach for her hand, but she moved it.

"Who's Kat?"

"Kat?" Isaak's voice sounded confused.

Dani was on a roll now. How dare he act dumb. She saw the text messages. "You told me you were not in a relationship, Isaak. This woman…Kat…or whoever she is, she seems to be mighty attached to you." Dani felt her lip tremble as she forced the words out.

Isaak appeared to be searching for the right words. "Kat's just a…."

"Friend? Friends don't have beds that get cold without them, Isaak." Dani closed her eyes and tried to get herself to calm down. Her life was spinning out of control in just a matter of minutes. One minute she was happier than she had been in a long time, and the next, she was so angry at him she could spit nails.

"We've had an open relationship, but we're not serious." Isaak was searching for the right words.

Not serious? Did he take her for a fool? Those messages looked pretty serious to her. There was no way she'd allow herself to be his little 'something on the side' while he shared his bed with another woman in the city. She wanted his whole heart or nothing at all. Better to break it off now than allow her heart to be devastated later. "I don't do casual, Isaak. I don't think this is going to work."

Isaak frowned at her statement. "You're just afraid to try." He was a little angry now too.

Dani sucked in her breath as if he had slapped her. She pushed away from the table and started to walk away from him. When she made it behind the bar, she looked at him with angry tears running down her face. She was angry at him, herself, and anyone who got in the way of her hasty retreat. "Goodbye, Isaak."

A few moments later, Jacob stepped out of the kitchen and saw Dani's demeanor. Without waiting for an explanation, he turned to Isaak. "You should go."

Isaak nodded and picked up his phone. He walked out the front door without looking back.

Chapter 17

Funny how quickly time moved when he only wanted it to slow down. It had been a few months since he had left. He had tried to get back into the swing of things when he returned to his everyday life. That was not as easy as he thought it would be. Isaak had left Vancouver a different man. Gone was his incessant need to have his pants completely wrinkle-free and his shirt uncomfortably starched. His time in the rainforest had made him realize life was too short to strive for absolute perfection.

Isaak was back at the Wildlife Adventure office at his desk. Now that he had returned, Angel expected a miracle from him. He had turned in several other articles, but Angel was still waiting for that one article that would change everything. That was sure easier said than done. Every time he tried to start off his article, he ended up deleting every word. Isaak was haunted by the tear-stained face of the only woman who had truly made him feel alive. Over and over, he tried to start and restart but only ended up staring at his computer screen. His cursor was blinking in its own secret code as his thoughts escaped him.

Isaak brought his hands to his eyes as if rubbing them would fix his problem. It hadn't all the times before. He had just another few hours before Angel would be breathing fire down his back. Isaak had put this off as long as he possibly could. "Maybe some coffee." He wasn't sure exactly how that would help, but it was a distraction.

He went to the back of the office, where the coffee counter was set up. Angel made sure the office always had a functioning coffee maker and plenty of supplies to make enough coffee to keep the writers happy. Isaak was standing at the counter, pouring his cup, when Angel called to him from her office.

"Isaak, a moment?"

"Sure." Isaak turned to the sound of her voice. He put the coffee pot down and moved toward her office door.

Angel was looking through a file folder on her desk. She looked up at Isaak as he entered. "Sit."

Isaak did as directed. "What's up?"

"Have you finished the story yet?"

He felt the guilt tug at him again. This article was important to his job, but his conscience wasn't allowing him to write it. What could he say? Angel was expecting an answer from him. "It's going," he half lied.

"Your writing has improved since your trip. Our readership has enjoyed the new articles, so you have that going in your favor, but they are still not the liquid gold this story could be. You know how important this article will be for your career, Isaak. You can't put it off any longer," cautioned Angel.

Isaak was preparing for another dress down, so he focused on the window behind her. As he did, he saw a flash of black feathers come down from the sky. He blinked to clear his eyes, thinking he must be losing his mind. When he looked out the window, this time, a raven landed on the windowsill outside. Isaak was taken aback, and Angel noticed.

She glanced at the window and didn't see anything unusual, then back to Isaak. "Something the matter, Isaak?"

Isaak focused back on Angel. "Just a bird."

Angel turned to look out the window again. "What bird?"

Isaak looked back at the window and saw that, indeed, the bird was gone. "It's nothing. I just thought I saw...." He shook his head distractedly, trying to unlodge the uneasy feeling he now had.

"Forget the bird. I need that article." Angel shook her head and tapped a pen on her desk calendar.

"Understood." Isaak stood up and walked to the door. He turned back to the window and saw the bird again. This time it made eye contact with him before it flew away. Isaak's heart dropped to his stomach. He pulled his phone out of his pocket and looked to see if Dani had replied to any of his messages. He hadn't heard from her since he'd returned to the city.

Anger and frustration washed over him. Damn it! He felt like tossing his phone across the room. She had her convictions, and she sure was pigheaded. If only she had let him explain more about Kat. When he came home from his trip, the first thing he did was cut all ties with the woman. Kat hadn't taken it well, but he didn't care. She had been told repeatedly that they were not in a relationship, and the woman had gone and ruined what could have been a good thing.

Liar. He chided himself. This wasn't Kat's fault. It was his. He should have been honest with Dani from the beginning. She had every right to be mad at him. Isaak remembered the hurt on her face, and he felt like a jackass ten times over. Dani didn't deserve to be treated like second best by any man or the other woman. If he had his way, he would always put her front and center. All he needed was one more chance to prove his love for her. If only he could figure out how to do that.

Isaak walked back to his desk and sat down. The article was still open on the screen before him. He rested his head on his hand and stared at it. "Come on, Isaak. You got this."

Isaak opened one of the folders on his desktop and started scrolling through the pictures. He saw a few of Dani, and a dull ache pulsed inside him. As he continued to push through them, he saw the one with the two ravens with their beaks close together, and he suddenly knew why he couldn't write the article. Isaak was writing the wrong one. There was only one article he wanted to write, and it started a whole different way.

Isaak pulled the article file from his desktop into the trashcan on the screen. Then Isaak opened up another screen and started to type.

When I started this assignment, I had one thing in mind, creating an adventure that would help me see the world through my reader's eyes. Instead, I saw it through hers.

I've spent most of my life inside the concrete walls I have cemented around me, safe in the fact that I would one day have everything I wanted. My definition of success was chasing the next story that would bring me even more prestige. Now, I realize the greatest reward of all is only found in the rush of wind through her hair, the way her eyes light up in the firelight, and the fierce way she protects the world that would be less vibrant without her.

I started this journey looking for the greatest story

of all, one filled with danger, adventure, and intrigue, but I find myself wanting to share the one that's truest to my heart. It all started with one bird who seemed to know what I needed before I was wise enough to figure it out for myself....

The moment Isaak started, his fingers flew over the keys. He poured his heart and soul into his piece, knowing it opened him up to all kinds of scrutiny. He didn't care if this was the piece Angel was looking for because if he didn't get these words out, Isaak felt like he would never be able to write another word again. He wrote about his adventures in the forest, from kayaking to fishing, to learning that the safety of the protected animals was important. Even to people who enjoyed the sport of hunting, there had to be rules that they all followed. To be a real outdoorsman or woman, it was essential that they leave the forest, the stream, and every habitat they crossed untouched when they were done visiting it. For a while, we humans had some use of that land. These animals were the ones who had proper domain there.

When he was finally done, Isaak took a printed copy to Angel and stood over her desk while she read it. The woman had no tells. That's probably why she always won on poker night. He couldn't tell if she liked it or not. When she got to the last line, Angel looked up at him with a serious expression.

"I have one question."

"What?" Isaak was nervous. He had never written this raw or real before. There was no politics, no hot trigger topic. This was simply an article that expressed the love of a man who had never truly known it existed.

"Where has this writer been?" Angel smiled. "It's brilliant. I think it will read very well, especially to our women readers."

"You think so?" Isaak almost felt like he had sweat pooling on his brow. He had been worried about her reaction.

"This is raw and real." Angel pursed her lips. "It's sad, though."

"What?" Isaak was suddenly worried that Angel wouldn't post the article.

"That your dumbass ruined a good thing before you even got home." Angel shook her head.

She was preaching to the choir. "You don't have to tell me. I already know."

Angel sat back in her chair and stared up at Isaak expectantly. "So what are you going to do about it?"

Isaak threw out his hands and shrugged. "What can I do? She won't talk to me."

"Maybe you're doing it wrong."

Isaak looked out the window and wished for once the raven was outside. "I'm afraid I'm just too late."

"Well, this is going to print in the next issue. Maybe she'll read it and come racing to your open arms." A dreamy smile crossed her face.

Isaak grimaced at the low chances of that happening. He had burned that bridge. Dani had already closed her heart to him. "Fat chance. I messed up bad." Isaak cleared his throat. "I think I'm going to call it a night."

"Good. You're burning the candle at both ends," teased Angel.

He shook his head. "You're one to talk," returned Isaak.

Angel snorted. "Get out of here already."

By the time Isaak finally made it home, it was time for him to hit the hay. It had been an exhausting week. He found himself in bed well before midnight, but his brain wouldn't turn off. While his room was dark, the city lights still illuminated it much greater than the skies under the canopy of a forest with the natural light from the stars above. Isaak already missed that starry darkness. Here in the city, they were lucky to see a smidge of stars in the sky. Their brilliance seemed dull compared to all the electric signs and overlit billboards scattered across the city.

"Caw!" came the sound of the raven as it landed on his windowsill.

Isaak released an exasperated sigh as he sat on the edge of the bed and stared at the raven. "She won't even return my calls. What do you want from me?"

"Caw!" answered the bird.

Maybe he still needed to prove himself to her. This was going to take more than a little technology. Dani would never be impressed with emails, texts or phone calls. He should have figured that out by now.

~*~

A few weeks later, Isaak found himself back to where it had all started. Standing outside the Blue Moon Bar, the moon shone down on him, and he smiled. Here the moon was brighter than any neon sign or cityscape. He had missed it.

His boots crunched on the snow as he walked across the parking lot. Was it even possible that the area was even more beautiful in the wintertime? Isaak wondered how the winter impacted the rainforest. Maybe if things went well, Dani might show it to him.

As he stepped through the bar's front door, he made sure to kick the snow from his boots. After the door closed behind him, Isaak took in the bar in front of him. It was fairly empty tonight. Isaak wondered if the area had less patronage in the wintertime. That would certainly make things harder for Dani and her father. Did they struggle to make ends meet? He and his mother had been there before too. It wasn't an easy place to dig oneself out of either.

Isaak stepped up to the bar where Jacob was drying a few glasses. He was half-afraid to open his mouth and say anything, but this was too important to chicken out of. "Is Dani here?"

Jacob snorted and set the glass down on the counter so hard that it was close to breaking. "No. And I wouldn't tell you if she was."

Isaak winced as the glass made contact with the counter. He deserved that, and he would be the first to admit that. He had screwed up royally. Hell, he had been punishing himself since the moment he left. Isaak couldn't remember the last time he had even gotten a full night's sleep. It wasn't until he found some nature sounds on an app on his phone that Isaak had even remotely been able to wind down at night.

Isaak drummed up the courage to move forward. If he had any hopes of getting on Dani's good side, he'd have to get past her father first. If he had hurt Dani half as bad as he hurt himself, he couldn't blame the man for being overprotective. "I know you have your reasons, but I need to talk to her." Isaak slid the magazine onto the bar, opened to the article with a picture of the two ravens on the top. The title read Aurora Skies.

Isaak was hoping the article would be enough for him to break through the wall here. If Jacob would just help him see Dani, maybe she would give him a chance to hear him out. The best prize in the world would be a second chance, a do-over of sorts. "Just read it, please."

"Fine," Jacob grunted in response before pulling

the magazine closer. His eyes were trained on the article as he read through it.

Isaak was nervous as Jacob read the lines that had taken months to pull out of him. The problem had been the topic. He had never found the passion inside him when he wrote. Isaak had always done what was expected and churned out one piece after another, completely polished and biased to the audience that paid the most money to read it. This article meant everything to him because Dani was everything to him. In the short span of a few days, the snarky defensive woman had crawled under his skin and changed him for life. She was everything he needed. If only she needed him too.

When Jacob was finished with the first full page, he looked up at Isaak, and a slow smile spread across his face. "I guess I was wrong about you after all."

Isaak held his hand up to deny his words. "No, you were right. I was an egotistical fool, but I'd like to think I've changed."

Jacob nodded his head slowly. "Looks that way."

"I just need a chance." One tiny chance. That was all he was asking for. Isaak couldn't move on until he had tried everything.

Jacob nodded to him again and passed the magazine back to him. "Got a piece of paper? Your GPS won't help you much where you're going."

Isaak gave him a helpless look before Jacob pulled out a paper napkin and started writing on it. "Here. Good luck. You're going to need it."

Isaak didn't plan on wasting any time. He took the napkin and bowed his head to Jacob before turning on his heel and heading right back out of the bar. His steps were almost too fast when he walked across the parking, for he almost lost his footing halfway across. Thankfully, he was able to right himself before falling on his backside. When he sat in the rental car, he opened the directions and tried to get them in his memory.

He drove the lone deserted lanes, taking the curves slowly. Isaak wanted to get there in one piece. The roads were icy, which was definitely not a good combination on a dark night in unfamiliar territory. The drive took longer than he wanted it to, and by the time he made it to her place, his fingers were wrapped so tight around the wheel that he was afraid they would never unclench.

Isaak was not surprised that Dani had chosen to live in seclusion. It may seem that way to most people, but Isaak knew that here she was constantly surrounded by mother nature. She probably had her favorite visitors every day, the furry kind that she fed a special diet to keep them healthy. As he scanned the area for a sign of any of these creatures, he was caught up by the amazing glowing lights of the Aurora Borealis that illuminated the sky. He had seen it before, but not in such an open sky. It was one of the most beautiful things he had ever seen, the kind of light that seemed to warm a person from the top of their heads to the bottom of their feet.

Isaak forced himself to turn back to the cabin. The rustic log cabin sat up on top of a bluff overlooking the water below. The lights were on behind the drawn curtains, so he knew Dani was still awake. Isaak made his way up the small path up to the cabin. He paused for a few seconds before stopping in front of the door. He was trying to find the resolve to face her no matter what response she gave him. Isaak raised his hand, took a breath, then knocked on the door. He listened for the shuffling of feet, and when he heard the small click of the door being unlocked, he took another deep breath.

Dani was standing in the doorway with a frown on her face the moment she saw him there. Even angry, she was a sight for sore eyes. "You. What are you doing here?"

Isaak shuffled from foot to foot nervously. He only had one shot at this, and he needed to make it count. "I just need to talk to you."

"Go away, Isaak." Dani started to close the door, but a raven cawed in the background. Dani's shoulders slumped in resignation. "Fine!"

Isaak looked over to see the raven perched on a nearby branch, then turned back to Dani. "I see he's been pestering you too." Why wasn't Isaak surprised?

"Every day. Wish he'd fly off." Dani crossed her arms over her chest and tilted her head.

"I never thought you'd say that." Isaak was concerned at her words. She was not in a good place. Was she wallowing in the same darkness he was?

"What do you want?" she let out an exasperated sigh.

"Read this." Isaak opened the magazine to his

article.

Dani looked at him in disbelief. "Are you kidding me?"

"Please." Isaak handed her the magazine and stepped back.

Dani's eyebrow rose. "And what are you going to do?"

Isaak shrugged. "I'll just take a walk."

"It's cold out there." She looked down at the article, then back at Isaak.

He waved off her concern. "I'll be fine."

Isaak walked to the bluff just down the hill from the cabin. There was a split rail fence that bordered the edge of the bluff to keep people from going too far for comfort. Isaak was surprised that Dani was so close to the ocean. She truly had the best of every world here. He understood why she wouldn't want to leave it. He thought about what it must be like to live life at a slower pace surrounded by such eternal beauty. The only thing that would make it better would be having someone he loved to share it with. Was it so wrong to want to share something like this with her? He would give up everything if she would just give him a chance.

As he stood there, he didn't hear Dani approach. Her steps were just as light as they had always been. He almost jumped out of his skin when her voice interrupted his thoughts.

"Did you mean it?"

Isaak turned to her. Under the aurora sky, she looked hopeful and vulnerable. Her feelings were raw and there for him to see. For the first time in months, Isaak felt like he may have a chance again at true love. "Every word. I love you, Dani."

Her eyes were filled with tears, but she had a wobbly smile on her face. "I love you too."

Isaak wasn't sure where this road would lead them. He was just happy that Dani let him on the trail beside her. He wiped away the tear on her cheek and leaned down to kiss her.

The two ravens landed on the fence near them. They crowed one last time and then took to the skies. And for once, Isaak felt like all the pieces of his life had finally fallen into place. His life had changed the minute he stepped into that bar and saw the sassy woman who stared him down so easily. She had taught him more about himself than he had learned the sum of his life, and he would be forever thankful for it.

Ever since childhood, Elissa Daye has enjoyed reading stories as an escape from life. When she was a teenager she started to write her own stories that kept her entertained when she ran out of books to read. When she was accepted into Illinois Summer School for the Arts in her Junior year of High School, she knew she wanted to become a writer. Elissa graduated from Illinois State University in December 1999 with a Bachelor of Science in Elementary Education and began her teaching career, hoping to find moments to write in her free time.

After seven years of teaching, Elissa decided to focus on her writing and made the decision to put her teaching years behind her so that she could create the stories she had always dreamed of. She is now happily married and a stay at home mom, who writes in every spare moment she can find, doing her best to master the art of multitasking to get everything accomplished.

Born in Northern Alabama, Karen Fuller learned to love the written word at the age of 12. She is a published author and generally writes Adult & Young Adult Paranormal Romance, and Young Adult Historical Romance under her given name, and writes children's middle-grade fiction under the pen name of K. G. Fuller. She's an award-winning author, a screenwriter, and she helps other authors further their careers.

www.ingramcontent.com/pod-product-compliance
Lightning Source LLC
Chambersburg PA
CBHW030304180626
46810CB00003B/910